Scission

Tim Winton was born in Perth in 1960 and has written novels, collections of stories, non-fiction and books for children. He has won the Miles Franklin Award four times, and been twice shortlisted for the Booker Prize, for *The Riders* (1995) and *Dirt Music* (2002).

Also by Tim Winton

Novels

An Open Swimmer

Shallows

That Eye, The Sky

In the Winter Dark

Cloudstreet

The Riders

Dirt Music

Breath

Stories

Minimum of Two

The Turning

Scission

Tim Winton

PICADOR

First published 1985 by McPhee Gribble Publishers Pty Ltd, Victoria, Australia,
in association with Penguin Books Australia Ltd,
with the assistance of the Literature Board of the Australia Council

First published in Great Britain 1993 by Picador as part of *Blood and Water*

This edition published 2003 by Picador
an imprint of Pan Macmillan Ltd
Pan Macmillan, 20 New Wharf Road, London N1 9RR
Basingstoke and Oxford
Associated companies throughout the world
www.panmacmillan.com

ISBN 978-0-330-41260-5

Copyright © Tim Winton 1985

All rights reserved. No part of this publication may be
reproduced, stored in or introduced into a retrieval system, or
transmitted, in any form, or by any means (electronic, mechanical,
photocopying, recording or otherwise) without the prior written
permission of the publisher. Any person who does any unauthorized
act in relation to this publication may be liable to criminal
prosecution and civil claims for damages.

9 8 7 6 5 4 3 2

A CIP catalogue record for this book is available from
the British Library.

Typeset by SX Composing DTP, Rayleigh, Essex
Printed in the UK by CPI Mackays, Chatham ME5 8TD

This book is sold subject to the condition that it shall not,
by way of trade or otherwise, be lent, re-sold, hired out,
or otherwise circulated without the publisher's prior consent
in any form of binding or cover other than that in which
it is published and without a similar condition including this
condition being imposed on the subsequent purchaser.

Visit **www.picador.com** to read more about all our books
and to buy them. You will also find features, author interviews and
news of any author events, and you can sign up for e-newsletters
so that you're always first to hear about our new releases.

this one is for Gonzo

Acknowledgements

Acknowledgement is made to the publication in which these stories first appeared: 'Secrets' in *Meanjin*, 1983; 'A Blow, A Kiss' in *Simply Living*, 1984; 'Getting Ahead' in *Island*, 1984; 'My Father's Axe' in *Australian Playboy*, 1983 (also winner of the 1983 State of Victoria Award); 'Wake' in *Quadrant*, 1982; 'Lantern Stalk' in the *Age Monthly Review*, 1984; 'Neighbours' in *Australian Short Stories*, 1985; 'A Measure of Eloquence' in the *Bulletin*, 1984; 'The Oppressed' in *Southern Review*, 1982; 'The Woman at the Well' in *Imprint*, 1982; and 'Scission' in *Westerly*, 1983.

The author thanks the Literature Board of the Australia Council for fellowships in 1983 and 1984.

Then Job answered and said,
    How long will ye vex my soul, and break me in pieces with words?

The Book of Job

The wounded surgeon plies the steel
That questions the distempered part;

T. S. Eliot, *East Coker*

Contents

Secrets – 1

A blow, a kiss – 7

Getting ahead – 15

My father's axe – 24

Wake – 36

Lantern stalk – 42

Thomas Awkner floats – 52

Wilderness – 62

Neighbours – 84

A measure of eloquence – 89

The oppressed – 102

The woman at the well – 114

Scission – 120

Secrets

Out the back of the new house, between the picket fence and a sheet of tin, Kylie found an egg. Her mother and Philip were inside. She heard them arguing and wished she still lived with her father. The yard was long and excitingly littered with fallen grapevines, a shed, lengths of timber and wire, and twitching shadows from big trees. It wasn't a new house, but it was new to her. She had been exploring the yard. The egg was white and warm-looking in its nest of dirt and down. Reaching in, she picked it up and found that it *was* warm. She looked back at the house. No one was watching. Something rose in her chest: now she knew what it was to have a secret.

At dinner her mother and Philip spoke quietly to one another and drank from the bottle she was only allowed to look at. Her mother was a tall woman with short hair like a boy. One of her front teeth had gone brown and it made Kylie wonder. She knew that Philip was Mum's new husband, only they weren't married. He smelt of cigarettes and moustache hairs; Kylie thought his feet were the shape of pasties.

When everything on her plate was gone, Kylie left the table. Because the loungeroom was a jungle of boxes and crates inside one of which was the TV, she went straight to her new room. She thought about the egg as she lay in bed. She was thinking about it when she fell asleep.

Next day, Kylie got up on to the fence and crabbed all around it looking into the neighbours' yards. The people behind had a little tin shed and a wired-up run against the fence in which hens and a puff-chested little rooster pecked and picked and scruffled. So, she thought, balanced on the splintery grey fence, that's where the egg comes from. She climbed down and checked behind the sheet of tin and found the egg safe but cold.

Later, she climbed one of the big trees in the yard, right up, from where she could observe the hens and the rooster next door. They were fat, white birds with big red combs and bright eyes. They clucked and preened and ruffled and Kylie grew to like them. She was angry when the piebald rooster beat them down to the ground and jumped on their backs, pecking and twisting their necks. All his colours were angry colours; he looked mean.

Inside the house Mum and Philip laughed or shouted and reminded her that Dad didn't live with them any more. It was good to have a secret from them, good to be the owner of something precious. Philip laughed at the things she said. Her mother only listened to her with a smile that said *you don't know a single true thing*.

Sometime in the afternoon, after shopping with her mother, Kylie found a second egg in the place between the fence and the tin. She saw, too, a flash of white beneath a mound of vine cuttings in the corner of the yard. She climbed her tree and waited. A hen, thinner and more raggedy than the others, emerged. She had a bloody comb and a furtive way of pecking the ground alertly and moving in nervous bursts. For some time, she poked and scratched about, fossicking snails and slugs out of the long grass, until Kylie saw her move across to the piece of tin and disappear.

Each day Kylie saw another egg added to the nest up the back. She saw the raggedy hen pecked and chased and kicked by the others next door, saw her slip between the pickets to escape. The secret became bigger every day. The holidays stretched on. Philip and her mother left her alone. She was happy. She sat on the fence, sharing the secret with the hen.

When they had first moved into this house on the leafy, quiet street, Philip had shown Kylie and her mother the round, galvanized tin cover of the bore well in the back of the yard. The sun winked off it in the mornings. Philip said it was thirty-six feet deep and very dangerous. Kylie was forbidden to lift the lid. It was off-limits. She was fascinated by it. Some afternoons she sat out under the grapevines with her photo album, turning pages and looking across every now and then at that glinting lid. It couldn't be seen from the back veranda; it was obscured by a banana tree and a leaning brick well.

In all her photographs, there was not one of her father. He had been the photographer in the family; he took photos of Kylie and her mother, Kylie and her friends, but he was always out of the picture, behind the camera. Sometimes she found herself looking for him in the pictures. Sometimes it was a game for her; at others she didn't realize she was doing it.

*

Two weeks passed. It was a sunny, quiet time. Ten eggs came to be secreted behind the piece of tin against the back fence. The hen began sitting on them. Kylie suspected something new would happen. She visited the scraggy, white hen every day to see her bright eyes, to smell her musty warmth. It was an important secret now. She sneaked kitchen scraps and canary food up the back each evening and lay awake in bed wondering what would happen.

It was at this time that Kylie began to lift the lid of the well. It was not heavy and it moved easily. Carefully, those mornings, shielded by the banana tree, she peered down into the cylindrical pit which smelt sweaty and dank. Right down at the bottom was something that looked like an engine with pipes leading from it. A narrow, rusty ladder went down the wall of the well. Slugs and spiderwebs clung to it.

One afternoon when Philip and her mother were locked in the big bedroom, laughing and making the bed bark on the boards, Kylie took her photo album outside to the well, opened the lid and, with the book stuffed into the waistband of her shorts, went down the ladder with slow, deliberate movements. Flecks of rust came away under her hands, and fell whispering a long way down. The ladder quivered. The sky was a blue disc above growing smaller and paler. She climbed down past the engine to the moist sand and sat with her back to the curving wall. She looked up. It was like being a drop of water in a straw or a piece of rice in a blowpipe – the kind boys stung her with at school. She heard the neighbours' rooster crowing, and the sound of the wind. She looked through her album. Pictures of her mother showed her looking away into the distance. Her long, wheaten hair blew in the wind or hung still and beautiful. It had been so long. Her mother never looked at the camera. Kylie saw herself, ugly and short and dark beside her. She grew cold and climbed out of the well.

It seemed a bit of an ordinary thing to have done when she got out. Nevertheless, she went down every day to sit and think or to flick through the album.

The hen sat on her eggs for three weeks. Kylie sat on the fence and gloated, looking into the chook house next door at the rooster and his scrabbling hens who did not know what was happening her side of the fence. She knew now that there would be chicks. The encylopaedia said so.

On nights when Philip and her mother had friends over, Kylie listened from the darkened hallway to their jokes that made no sense. Through the crack between door and jamb she saw them touching each other beneath the table, and she wanted to know – right then – why her father and mother did not live together with her. It was something she was not allowed to know. She went back to her room and looked at the only picture in her album where her smile told her that there was something she knew that the photographer didn't. She couldn't remember what it was; it was a whole year ago. The photo was a shot from way back in kindergarten. She was small, dark-haired, with her hands propping up her face. She held the pictures close to her face. It made her confident. It made her think Philip and her mother were stupid. It stopped her from feeling lonely.

Philip caught her down the well on a Sunday afternoon. He had decided to weed the garden at last; she wasn't prepared for it. One moment she was alone with the must, the next, the well was full of Philip's shout. He came down and dragged her out. He hit her. He told her he was buying a padlock in the morning.

That evening the chicks hatched in the space between the sheet of tin and the back fence – ten of them. At dusk, Kylie put them into a cardboard box and dropped them down the well. The hen squawked insanely around the yard, throwing itself about, knocking things over, creating such a frightening noise that Kylie chased it and hit it with a piece of wood and, while it was still stunned, dropped it, too, down the dry well. She slumped down on the lid and began to cry. The back light came on. Philip came out to get her.

Before bed, Kylie took her photograph – the knowing one – from its place in the album, and with a pair of scissors, cut off her head and poked it through a hole in the flyscreen of the window.

A blow, a kiss

Despite their bad luck, Albie had enjoyed the night. Just the pipe smell of his father and the warmth of him in the truck's cab beside him was enough. It did not matter that they had caught ten salmon and buried them in the sand for safe keeping and not found them again. The Tilley lamp tinkled, cooling between his feet on the floor of the cab. Ahead, the unlit road rolled out.

A motorcycle whipped past, going their way. Albie saw the small red light for a moment and then it was gone.

'He's flying,' his father murmured.

'Yeah.' Albie felt his chin on his chest. He heard the lamp tinkle. His eyes closed. He looked up again, felt himself plummeting forward, heard his father pumping the brakes.

'He's down!' bellowed his father.

Albie pulled himself away from the windscreen. His father was already out of the cab and in the vortex of the headlights. On the road, the motorcycle was sprawled, intertwined with the rider, an ugly spillage. Against the blackness of the machine and leather, Albie saw blood. He did not move on the seat. He held the Tilley lamp hard between his feet; he had not let it fall and break.

His father pulled the machine from the man who

groaned. He took the helmet off. He held up the man's hands. They were the colour of bleeding pork. Albie had never seen so much human blood, though he had seen cut pigs and jugulars of salmon cannoning red on white sand. Groans became shouts. Without warning, the fallen man lashed out at Albie's father and pulled him down to the ground by the ears and the two men locked limbs, and rolled on the bloody bitumen in the headlights of the truck. Albie did not move. He held the Tilley lamp tight until his thighs ached. He heard the wet sound of fists connecting. Crickets and the quiet idle of the engine underlay this noise. Beyond the grovelling men, past the point of the truck's headlights, there was only darkness. In a moment there was quiet. Crickets chanted. The engine idled.

'Albie!'

Albie slid out of the cab as soon as he heard his father's voice. Every line and feature was stark in the glare. Blood ran from his father's lips. The fallen rider lay, gored jaws apart, beneath him.

'Come here, Albie.' His father motioned with a free hand. Albie smelt blood, and beer and petrol and hot metal. He saw a translucent disc on his father's cheek and for a moment he thought it was a tear but it was a fish scale. 'He's unconscious. We shouldn't move him. I'll have to call for help. Come over further. Now get on him.' Albie was astride the bleeding, still man. 'Put your feet on his hands. He won't move. He's out.' Albie wondered why it was necessary to sit on a man who was not going to move. He looked at the blood streaming from his father's lips. 'He's in shock – he didn't know what he was doing,' his father said. 'I won't be long – stay put.'

Albie felt his shoulder briefly squeezed and heard his

father's boots mashing back to the truck. The lights veered from him and the truck passed and the tail-lights became tiny red points, eyes that closed and left him with the dark. He heard the man's breathing, felt the rise and fall of leather, listened to the cricket hymns, wondering what should be done, how he should behave towards this man who had struck his father. In the dark, he could not see the places where skin had been pared away. He saw no human blood, but he could smell it.

'He was only helping you,' he said to the man. The leather jacket groaned beneath him. Albie wondered what his mother would be doing. Probably ringing Sergeant Fobles, he thought; she'll be angry and blame Dad, kiss us. Albie knew she would use her kisses like blows: punishment for them.

The leather jacket was wet in parts and torn. It shocked him that leather should rip like that; it was the strongest stuff there was, and only time and sweat and constant fatigue could waste it, not those few seconds when that single tail-light disappeared and this man skittered along the road like a moist piece of moss.

'You're lucky we were here,' he said, shifting position on the mount. 'You're lucky my Dad's going for help.'

Town was only twenty minutes' drive from the coast. Farmland stretched right to the high-water mark. Albie had seen cattle on the beaches, wallowing in the surf. He hoped his father found a farm with a phone.

'Come on, Dad. Come on, Dad. Come on, Dad.' He often prayed to his father in his absence. God, he decided, was just like his Dad, only bigger. It was easier to pray to him and hope God got the message on relay.

'Dad?'

Albie flinched. The injured man had spoken.
'Dad?'
Albie's body shrank into itself. He waited for the man to move, to attack.
'Dad?'
'Yes?' Albie whispered. His throat was full of heart.
'Oh. Oh, Dad, I'm sorry. Was coming back.'
Albie listened as the man began to weep; he rode the man's sobs, high on his chest, and it hurt him to hear. Like the sound of a tractor engine turning over on a dying battery.

'It's all right,' Albie said to him, 'it's all right.' The sobbing continued, jogging him, making the leather groan and the seat of his pants hot until Albie thought he might be sick or get up and run away into the bush at the side of the road.

But he did not run. He bent down and kissed the wet, prickled face. The sobbing stopped. Even the crickets paused. Albie tasted salt, felt a jumble of things lurching in him; he felt not sick, just full.

It was that moment when Albie began to worry that the man might die.

The lights forking out over the crown of the hill took him by surprise. He watched them dip and sweep, disappear and reappear until he could hear the sound of the truck's engine.

In the piercing white light of the truck's lamps, as it stopped dead with a shriek of brakes, Albie knew what it must be to be a rabbit, powerless, snowblind, vulnerable to atrocity. The light seemed to ricochet inside his head, confounding him. He heard his father's boots.

'You all right? There's blood on your face!'

Albie felt himself swept up into his father's arms; he yielded to it. His father hugged him, touched his cheeks with his fingers and his tobacco breath. On his own feet again, Albie found his voice and asked, 'Is he going to die?'

'Dunno,' his father said, 'I don't know enough about it.'

'Oh.'

'There's no phones. I should've known in the first place. Man'd have to be an idiot. We'll take him in ourselves like we should've anyhow.'

'We didn't want to move him.'

'Yeah.' His father seemed to take comfort in this.

Albie tried to stay awake in the warm cab, seduced by the smell of his father and the crooning note of the engine. The sweat had dried on him. His arms still ached. He had never lifted anything so heavy, so awkward as that fallen motorcyclist. They had tried to get his contorted, cold machine in too, but had to leave it at the roadside. Every few minutes, Albie turned to see through the window the shape of the injured man beneath the tarpaulin on the tray beside the rods and sacks and engine parts.

He held the Tilley lamp hard between his heels. It kept him awake, a duty.

'Should've known better,' his father muttered. The featureless road wandered left and right, studded with the eyes of beer cans, mile pegs, rabbits.

Somewhere in his fog of fatigue, Albie hoped his mother would understand. She loved them; she didn't like them to be late.

Town was mostly asleep at this time of night. Only the pub and the petrol station were open. It was a fuel town at night, a farm town by day. As they pulled into the sudden brilliance of the petrol station tarmac, Albie saw Mr Stevens wave to his father, a wave without hands. His father got out. After a moment, Mr Stevens came over. Albie listened.

'That's Wilf Beacon's boy,' Mr Stevens said, peering in the back at the man on the tray beneath the tarp. 'Dead?'

'No.'

Albie wished his father would check. He was afraid. But he saw the tarp rising and falling.

'Where's Beacon, then?'

'Across the road.'

Albie knew that in this town 'across the road' meant in the pub. The pub frightened Albie. From out on the veranda, it was a roar, a sour smell, unknown.

His father poked his head in the window. 'Stay here, son.'

Not long after, Albie saw two men stumble out on to the pub veranda. One was his father. The other man had him by the throat and his father had the man's forelock in his fist. Shouting. Albie saw his father hit the man in the chest. The man fell to his knees. His father helped him up and they came across the road to Stevens' Garage.

'Just pull yourself together,' he heard his father say with a harshness that made his skin prickle.

'Where's his suitcase? He had a sleeping bag! You've done 'im over! What've you been doin' to my boy?'

'Pickin' him up off the side of the road. He's drunk like you. He's hurt, you bloody idiot!'

Albie hated that man. He couldn't remember seeing him before. He was not a farmer. Might have been a farm hand for someone he didn't know. He didn't care; he hated him.

He wanted the man to see his son, and to weep like the son had wept out on the road with that hopeless starter motor sound in the dark.

His father shoved the man around to the back of the truck. Albie's insteps were cold from pressing against the lamp. He watched through the grimy little back window. The man staggered up on to the tray and knelt with a thud beside the body under the tarp.

'Little coward. Leave a man alone. Own father. Own father.' The rider's bloody face was immobile. The old man's hands touched it, lifted the head off the truck tray. 'And what've yer got to say for yerself? They bring yer back to *me*!' The sound of the rider's head being dropped on to the metal tray vibrated through the whole truck like the sound of a mallee root being tossed in. Again. Whump. The father beat his son's head against the tray. Albie's father looked helpless, did not move.

Albie got out. The flat bed of the truck resounded again. The jumble inside Albie pushed upward; he wanted to be sick. He snatched the Tilley lamp by the handle. He heard the startled voice of his father. He swung the lamp up and over, a bowling movement. Glass and sound and splintery light happened all at once and his father had hold of him as the drunk old man lay still on his son, stinking of beer and kerosene.

As they turned off the bitumen road into their own run of gravel to the yellow-lit house down in the valley, Albie ended the silence with a question. He was startled by his own toneless delivery.

'Why did that man hit his son for getting hurt?'

His father sighed. He sounded relieved that the silence was finished. 'I don't know, boy.'

'Would you do that to me?'

The truck slewed and stopped.

'Lord no. God A'mighty, no!'

'He was going home,' Albie said.

His father's mouth moved. He reached out and put his knuckles to Albie's cheek, left them there for a long time, as though still waiting for words to come. 'Sorry about the salmon,' he said at last, 'I should've known better.'

The truck moved forward again. Albie felt those knuckles on his cheek still and knew, full to bursting, that that was how God would touch someone. He neither moved nor spoke, and the truck trundled on.

Getting ahead

for Simon

It was three years after Dad died that Mum started to get ideas, and it nearly drove the five of us mad. After dinner, when all the pots and plates were washed, dried, inspected and put away, and the smallies put to bed, Jilly and I would do our homework and Mum would get thinking. She was like a broody hen sitting there in the corner of the sofa on her clutch of ideas, keeping them warm. Dad was the one with all the ideas before that, but all of them were lousy. It took Mum a few nights to come up with hers, and without a word one evening she got up, wrote them on a Scott Towel and stuck them to the door of the fridge.

> BE HEALTHY
> BE ORGANIZED
> BE CAREFUL
> GET AHEAD

We were dumbfounded. No one in our home had done anything like that before. Soon afterwards, she went out and bought a Dymo labeller (all the rage then) with the savings in the Vegemite jar in the cupboard. And then things started to happen. Labels: warnings, reminders, instructions appeared on everything. WASH HANDS! said the cistern in the outhouse. SHUT DOOR! cried everything with hinges. On our bedheads, adhesive checklists appeared in our absence: who to pray for, duties to be done, cautionary notices. Mum began to develop powerful wrists from punching out those sticky messages. You could hear the grot-grot sound of the pistol-like gadget all over the house.

She was a big woman, my mother. In poor light she resembled an untidy stack of tea-chests. She rumbled about the house at night checking us in our beds, not sleeping herself until Mahoney's rooster started to crow. We always liked the Mahoneys despite the rooster. Mrs Mahoney had what Mum called 'a generous bosom'; she was a good neighbour. Mum ironed and mended and we left her in bed when we got up for school in the mornings. She ironed and mended. And three years after the old man turned yellow and died, she got to thinking as well.

It wasn't long before the chief subject of conversation became getting ahead. Jilly and I were old enough to understand and too young to contradict. (That was another thing she said.) One night when we were working on our books, Mum ruffled herself in the corner of the sofa, putting her upper teeth in, and said, 'You've gotta get ahead.' We stopped work and looked at her gazing into the fire. 'You've got to find some way of getting ahead. You can't stand still.'

She said this once or twice a night for a whole week. Jilly and I thought she was going mental. Only mental people and teachers repeated themselves like that. But at the end of the week she looked into the fire and said: 'You know, kids, there's only two things more I'd like to try out in this life,' as if she'd done pretty well everything else; 'First, I'd like to see how long I could live off a packet of Jatz and my own wits in the desert, and second, I'd like to be a landlady.'

'I'd like to be a policeman,' I said, relieved that she hadn't gone mental after all.

'I'd like to be blonde,' Jilly said, holding out a lock of her carroty hair.

'But I'm too old for the desert,' Mum continued, as though we hadn't spoken. 'So, we're gonna get into real estate.'

Jilly and I exchanged looks of deep disturbance.

'We've got no money,' I said.

'We don't need it. We got a house. It's assets.'

Jilly wedged an elbow between my ribs. Mum took her teeth out and held them like they were a pair of specs and she was Julius Sumner Miller gazing into the fire and not our old Mum. 'We'll rent this place out.'

'But Mum,' I said hoarsely, 'there's six of us in it already.' There was no way I could believe she was serious. It was a two-bedroom state house. Not flash, not well painted, not well furnished, and as far as I was concerned, not available. Five of us, I thought, there's Maxford (me), Jilly, Eddy, Edie and Millicent; the smallies in Mum's room, Jilly and me in the other.

'We'll move into a flat.'

'A flat!' Jilly cried. Flats were where you got yelled at from balconies as you cut across the mangy lawns on your way to school. Flats were where ladies without husbands had to live. Flats had no backyards.

'Just for a while,' Mum said.

'How long?' I asked.

'It's just until we get ahead,' she said.

The flat had a bedroom, a living room, a kitchen and a bathroom/toilet/laundry (most confusing for the smallies) and we loathed it. Mum calculated we'd be making fifteen dollars a week on top of her pension, and all the time that we lived like refugees sleeping on the floor of that flat, aching for garden space, cubby space, fences to vault, dogs and bobtails to tangle with, I kept that fifteen dollars in mind. Our tenant, the person who rented our house, was a senile old woman who smelt of cat-pee and was called Mrs Marsdale. It took her a long time to answer the ad in the paper. We chose her because she was the only one who did. We didn't like her smell. Mum didn't care for her name. Millicent cried when we moved out.

'It's only till we get ahead,' Mum would say, as if to convince herself too. 'We're saving, we're saving.' It used to be a lullaby for the smallies, long, low, sweet.

But it was lousy in the flat. We didn't open the door to anyone except Mum in case the Health Inspector got on to us for overcrowding or the landlord saw Mum's Dymo labels all over the place, like PRESS HARD TWICE in the toilet, and MUMMY LOVES YOU policing the pantry door. The fridge had become scarfaced and confounding as Mum's old and new messages to us and herself and God (she had started praying in Dymo which, I suppose, is like doing it in tongues) accumulated day by day. We survived like this for months, clattering along balconies, passing our old place on the way to school for a look at how run-down the garden had become, at how many cats seemed to congregate on the veranda now, and coming home each afternoon to see our Mum knitting by the smelly kero heater with her teeth out trying not to look disgusted about being a landlady getting ahead.

The rent never seemed to arrive. One evening when all the others – even Jilly – were asleep on their mattresses on the floor, Mum sat beside me at the table where I was skirmishing with algebra, trying for the teacher's sake to pretend that x was the number 2 in disguise, and said:

'Will you come with me to the house tomorrow, after school?' There was a weighty tone in her voice, the kind that grown-ups reserved for other grown-ups.

'Course,' I said lumpily. 'What's up?'

'Oh,' she murmured, 'tenant problems.'

'Oh,' I replied, as if it was all too clear and much too commonplace.

Mrs Marsdale didn't seem to resent our inspection of the house. We exchanged good days and how-do-you-dos; she didn't seem to mind at all. In fact, I'm not even sure if she was really aware of our being there. She seemed to be in a kind of crooning, half-animated coma. She fell over bits of furniture as she spoke to them. She scratched herself. She scared me witless.

The house was a disappointment. The sofa looked as though someone had taken to it with a rasp. The floor was mulched with Kitty Litter, wet newspapers and wads of phlegmy cotton. Stacks of newspapers and magazines threatened to fall from every corner. Shopping trollies, bicycle wheels, steel buckets, a NO PARKING sign. And no sign of the three months' rent Mum had come to collect.

'Mrs Marsdale,' I heard my mother say as I discreetly picked a piece of blue meat from between my toes. 'Mrs Marsdale, I . . .'

I caught sight of her looking up at the ceiling where ugly

brown stains had appeared in our absence. 'Mrs Marsdale, is the roof leaking?' Mrs Marsdale continued her ecstasy of falling and muttering. 'Maxford,' Mum said, 'get the ladder.'

I went out to the shed for the ladder as Mum tried to hail Mrs Marsdale. When we got up into the ceiling, we found a colony of wild-eyed cats hissing at us from the farthest corners of the darkness. I heard a glottal exclamation from my Mum. She dragged me down the ladder and out the front door.

'There's worse than that,' she said as we walked home. She looked shocked and grey. 'I have reason to believe that our outhouse hasn't been used since Mrs . . . since our tenant moved in.'

'But Mum . . .'

'A woman can tell things about a bathtub the likes of a clean boy like you would never understand. It's because the toilet is a long way up the backyard. It's a long way, I'll grant it, but there's limits to what your mother'll tolerate, Maxford.'

'It's the most exasperating thing,' she said that night as the smallies brawled from one end of the room to the other with a frisbee. 'I can't understand the ways of some people. It's not right. Oh, oh . . .' And in the midst of that tiny battleground of mattresses and rioting bodies, I thought she was going to cry. The cracking, sliding look on her face lasted a full five seconds before she said: 'Well, I'll just have to appeal to her sense of decency.' The world was a stable place again; the Laws still held. Our Mum did not cry.

In the calm after tea, by the smelly heater, Jilly and I watched her punch out an honest, forthright letter on the Dymo, a long blue strip that coiled at her feet: grot-grot,

grot-grot, grot-grot. She was still at it when we flopped on our mattresses and went to sleep.

'. . . just until we get ahead . . .' I heard her murmur as I dropped off.

The long blue adhesive salutation Mum stuck to the front door seemed to go unheeded. Mum went round during the day, just to watch the cats from the footpath and to think. In the flat she muttered and scowled and thumped the kitchen sink.

'Then it's persuasion,' she murmured late in the evening, polishing her teeth with cotton buds by the heater. I was hard at work with my algebra and paid no attention.

So, walking in the warm dark towards our old house the next night, I had no idea what it was we were doing.

Dogs barked all over the suburb. A few sprinklers tinkled. There was no light on at our place and none in the neighbours' either. It was very late. I followed the jumbling shape of my Mum up the side of the house and out to the back shed. She gave me a shovel.

'Dig,' she whispered.

'Where?'

'Anywhere.'

I dug, on my knees in the dewy grass. She kept watch. There was no light and no noise from the house. On the back veranda, cats watched us, starlight catching in their eyes. I dug deep, narrow holes. Four of them. Then suddenly we left. I was put to bed.

Next day after school, Mum had four potted saplings standing on the sink. She was acting most peculiar, drinking tea, humming. 'My investments,' she called them. That night she got me out of bed at midnight. We walked across to our old place again, only this time I carried two potted saplings and a bellyful of dread. Again, no lights, no signs of wakefulness from inside. Our holes were still there with their gentle mounds of sand.

'Get the big spanner from the shed,' she whispered. I did. 'Now,' she hissed, 'catch cats.' And then I knew.

I slunk across the yard. 'Puss-puss-puss.' A black cat appeared from the darkness, slowly coming to my call. It spat and scratched when I grabbed it by the scuff of the neck and delivered it to Mum. She hit it on the head with the big spanner and dropped it into the nearest hole.

'One down,' she said. Needlessly, I thought. I went back to kitty-kittying, thinking: So this is persuasion. Cats came slower and slower as time passed, but the darkness continued to yield them up all the same. Mum bedded each hole with four or five cats and planted a sapling in each, squashing down the soil around them with her boots. All except the fourth. She wanted to be sure we got every single cat. I prowled up and down, tired now, and feeling wretched about the cats. After a while it was obvious that there were no more. It was at that moment that a sound behind me caused me to go rocky with fright. I saw Mum's jaw, long and white, down in the dark. She looked shocked.

'Psst!'

I could not move. I was certain the blood had halted in my veins. I heard the clack of Mum's upper plate. With great effort, I turned to face the noise. Mum turned too. There were the big white arms of Mrs Mahoney on the fence. Our neighbour, Mrs Mahoney. She was looking at us very carefully. Her eyes seemed to glow in the dark. My head was pregnant with the consequences of being caught in the act.

Mrs Mahoney lifted a finger and motioned for us to come closer. We inched forward. I saw her eyes clearly. They were no-nonsense eyes. She pointed them at my Mum. I wanted to cry.

'Yes?' my poor Mum said.

'There's one under the woodpile.'

All the way home in the dark an hour later, Mum sang hymns and kicked stones in a clatter down the street as if nothing in the world could be a danger or a problem. It was as though she had gotten drunk on Mrs Mahoney's cup of tea. Mrs Mahoney had told us of Mrs Marsdale's disappearance. 'Two days she's bin gone. Ever since you came round for the rent. Left the cats and all.' The fact that Mrs Marsdale had gone without paying didn't worry Mum on that warm, dead-of-night walk home. The state of our old house, the brown cat-piddle ceilings, the gutless furniture, the filth didn't bother her. The fact that we were not ahead was no burden to bear. The house was empty. We were moving home. Mrs Mahoney was a sport.

'And we've got ahead, really,' she said. 'We've got four new trees.' Which was true. And still is. They're the best thing about the place. Ask my kids.

My father's axe

1

Just now I discover the axe gone. I look everywhere inside and outside the house, front and back, but it is gone. It has been on my front veranda since the new truckload of wood arrived and was dumped so intelligently over my front lawn. Jamie says he doesn't know where the axe is and I believe him; he won't chop wood any more. Elaine hasn't seen it; it's men's business, she says. No, it's not anywhere. But who would steal an axe in this neighbourhood, this street where I grew up and have lived much of my life? No one steals on this street. Not an axe.

It is my father's axe.

I used to watch him chop with it when we drove the old Morris and the trailer outside the town limits to gather wood. He would tie a thick, short bar of wood to the end of forty feet of rope and swing it about his head like a lasso and the sound it made was the whoop! of the headmaster's cane you heard when you walked past his office. My father sent the piece of wood high into the crown of a dead sheoak and when it snarled in the stark, grey limbs he would wrap the rope around his waist and then around his big, freckled arms, and he would pass me his grey hat with bound hands and tell me to stand right back near the Morris with my mother who poured tea from a Thermos flask. And he pulled. I heard his body grunt and saw his red arms whiten, and the tree's crown quivered and rocked and he added to the motion, tugging, jerking, gasping until the whole bush cracked open and birds burst from all the trees around and the dead, grey crown of the sheoak teetered and toppled to the earth, chased by a shower of twigs and bark. My mother and I cheered and my father ambled over, arms glistening, to drink the tea that tasted faintly of coffee and the rubber seal of the Thermos. Rested, he would then dismember the brittle tree with graceful swings of his axe and later I would saw with him on the bowman saw and have my knees showered with white, pulpy dust.

He could swing an axe, my father.

And that axe is gone.

He taught me how to split wood though I could never do it like him, those long, rhythmic, semicircular movements like a ballet dancer's warm-up; I'm a left-hander, a mollydooker he called me, and I chop in short, jabby strokes which do the job but are somehow less graceful.

When my father began to leave us for long periods for his work – he sold things – he left me with the responsibility of fuelling the home. It gave me pride to know that our hot water, my mother's cooking, the living-room fire depended upon me, and my mother called me the man of the house, which frightened me a little. Short, winter afternoons I spent up the back splitting pine for kindling, long, fragrant spines with neat grain, and I opened up the heads of mill-ends and sawn blocks of sheoak my father brought home. Sometimes in the trance of movement and exertion I imagined the blocks of wood as teachers' heads. It was pleasurable work when the wood was dry and the grain good and when I kept the old Kelly axe sharp. I learnt to swing single-handed, to fit wedges into stubborn grain, to negotiate knots with resolve, and the chopping warmed me as I stripped to my singlet and worked until I was ankle-deep in split, open wood and my breath steamed out in front of me with each righteous grunt.

Once, a mouse half caught itself in a trap in the laundry beneath the big stone trough and my mother asked me to kill it, to put it out of its misery, she said. Obediently, I carried the threshing mouse in the trap at arm's length right up to the back of the yard. How to kill a mouse? Wring its neck? Too small. Drown it? In what? I put it on the burred block and hit it with the flat of my axe. It made no noise but it left a speck of red on my knee.

Another time my father, leaving again for a long trip, began softly to weep on our front step. My mother did not see because she was inside finding him some fruit. I saw my father ball his handkerchief up and bite on it to muffle his sobs and I left him there and ran through the house and up to the woodpile where I shattered great blocks of sheoak until it was dark and my arms gave out. In the dark I stacked wood into the buckled shed and listened to my mother calling.

I broke the handle of that axe once, on a camping trip; it was good hickory and I was afraid to tell him. I always broke my father's tools, blunted his chisels, bent his nails. I have never been a handyman like my father. He made things and repaired things and I watched but did not see the need to learn because I knew my father would always be. If I needed something built, something done, there was my father and he protected me.

When I was eight or nine he took my mother and me to

a beach shack at a rivermouth up north. The shack was infested with rats and I lay awake nights listening to them until dawn when my father came and roused me and we went down to haul the craypots. The onshore reefs at low tide were bare, clicking and bubbling in the early sun, and octopuses gangled across exposed rock, lolloping from hole to hole. We caught them for bait; my father caught them and I carried them in the bucket with the tight lid and looked at my face in the still tidal pools that bristled with kelp. But it was not so peaceful at high tide when the swells burst on the upper lip of the reef and cascaded walls of foam that rushed in upon us and rocked us with their force. The water reached my waist though it was only knee-deep for my father. He taught me to brace myself side-on to the waves and find footholds in the reef and I hugged his leg and felt his immovable stance and moulded myself to him. At the edge of the reef I coiled the rope that he hauled up and held the hessian bag as he opened the heavy, timber-slatted pots; he dropped the crays in and I heard their tweaking cries and felt them grovelling against my legs.

During the day my mother read *They're a Weird Mob* and ate raisins and cold crayfish dipped in red vinegar. We played Scrabble and it did not bother me that my father lost.

Lost his axe. Who could have stolen such a worthless thing? The handle is split and taped and the head bears the scars of years; why even look at it?

One night on that holiday a rat set off a trap on the rafter above my bed. My father used to tie the traps to the rafters to prevent the rats from carrying them off. It went off in the middle of the night with a snap like a small fire cracker and in the dark I sensed something moving above me and something warm touched my forehead. I lay still and did not scream because I knew my father would come. Perhaps I did scream in the end, I don't know. But he came, and he lit the Tilley lamp and chuckled and, yes, that was when I screamed. The rat, suspended by six feet of cord, swung in an arc across my bed with the long, hairy whip of tail trailing a foot above my nose. The body still flexed and struggled. My father took it down and went outside with its silhouette in the lamplight in front of him. My mother screamed; there was a drop of blood on my forehead. It was just like *The Pit and the Pendulum*, I said. We had recently seen the film and she had found the book in the library and read it to me for a week at bedtime. Yes, she said with a grim smile, wiping my forehead, and I had nightmares about that long, hairy blade above my throat and saw it snatched away by my father's red arms. In the morning I saw outside that the axe head was dull with blood. After that I often had dreams in which my father rescued me. One was a dream about a burning house – our house, the one I still live in with Elaine and Jamie – and I was trapped inside, hair and bedclothes afire and my father splintered the door with an axe blow and fought his way in and carried me out in those red arms.

My father. He said little. He never won at Scrabble, so it seems he never even stored words up for himself. We never spoke much. It was my mother and I who carried on the long conversations; she knew odd facts, quiz shows on television were her texts. I told her my problems. But with my father I just stood, and we watched each other. Sometimes he looked at me with disappointment, and other times I looked at him the same way. He hammered big nails in straight and kissed me goodnight and goodbye and hello until I was fourteen and learnt to be ashamed of it and evade it.

When his back stiffened with age he chopped wood less and I wielded the axe more. He sat by the woodpile and sometimes stacked, though mostly he just sat with a thoughtful look on his face. As I grew older my time contracted around me like a shrinking shirt and I chopped wood hurriedly, often finishing before the old man had a chance to come out and sit down.

Then I met Elaine and we married and I left home. For years I went back once a week to chop wood for the old man while Elaine and my mother sat at the Laminex table in the kitchen listening to the tick of the stove. I tried to get my parents interested in electric heating and cooking like most people in the city, but my father did not care for it. He was stubborn and so I continued to split wood for him once a week while he became a frail, old man and his arms lost their ruddiness and went pasty and the flesh lost its grip upon the bones of his forearms. He looked at me in disappointment every week like an old man will, but I came over on Sundays, even when we had Jamie to look after, so he didn't have cause to be that way.

Jamie got old enough to use an axe and I taught him how. He was keen at first, though careless, and he blunted the edge quite often which angered me. I got him to chop wood for his grandfather and dropped him there on Sunday afternoons. I had a telephone installed in their house, though they complained about the colour, and I spoke to my mother sometimes on the phone, just to please her. My father never spoke on the phone. Still doesn't.

Then my mother had her stroke and Jamie began demanding to be paid for woodchopping and Elaine went twice a week to cook and clean for them and I decided on the Home. My mother and father moved out and we moved in and sold our own house. I thought about getting the place converted to electricity but the Home was expensive and Elaine came to enjoy cooking on the old combustion stove and it was worth paying Jamie a little to chop wood. Until recently. Now he won't even do it for money. He is lazier than me.

Still, it was only an old axe.

2

Elaine sleeps softly beside me, her big wide buttocks warm against my legs. The house is quiet; it was always quiet, even when my parents and I lived there. No one ever raised their voice at me in this house, except now my wife and son.

It is hard to sleep, hard, so difficult. Black moves about me and in me and is on me, so black. Fresh, bittersweet, the smell of split wood: hard, splintery jarrah, clean, moist sheoak, hard, fibrous white gum, the shick! of sundering pine. All my muscles sing, a chorus of effort, as I chop quickly, throwing chunks aside, wiping flecks and chips from my chin. Sweat sheets across my eyes and I chop harder, opening big round sawn blocks of sheoak like pies in neat wedged sections. Harder. And my feet begin to lift as I swing the axe high over my shoulder. I strike it home and regain equilibrium. As I swing again my feet lift further and I feel as though I might float up, borne away by the axe above my head, as though it is a helium balloon. No, I don't want to lift up! I drag on the hickory handle, downwards, and I win and drag harder and it gains momentum and begins a slow-motion arc of descent towards the porous surface of the wood and then, half-way down, the axe-head shears off the end of the handle so slowly, so painfully slow that I could take a hold of it four or five times to stop it. In a slow, tumbling trajectory it sails across the woodheap and unseats my father's head from his shoulders and travels on out of sight as my father's head rolls on to the heap, eyes towards me, transfixed at the moment of scission in a squint of disappointment.

I feel a warm dob on my forehead; I do not scream, have never needed to.

The sheets are wet and the light is on and Elaine has me by the shoulder and her left breast points down at my glistening chest.

'What's the matter?' she says, wiping my brow with the back of her hand. 'You were yelling.'

'A dream,' I croak.

3

Morning sun slants across the pickets at me as I fossick about in the long grass beside the shed finding the skeleton of a wren but nothing else. I shuffle around the shed, picking through the chips and splinters and slivers of wood around the chopping block, see the deep welts in the block where the axe has been, but no axe. In the front yard, as neighbours pass, I scrabble in the pile of new wood, digging into its heart, tossing pieces aside until there is nothing but yellowing grass and a few impassive slaters. Out in the backyard again I amble about shaking my head and putting my hands in my pockets and taking them out again. Elaine is at work. Jamie at school. I have rung the office and told them

I won't be in. All morning I mope in the yard, waiting for something to happen, absurdly, expecting the axe to show like a prodigal son. Nothing.

Going inside at noon I notice a deep trench in the veranda post by the back door; it is deep and wide as a heavy axe-blow and I feel the inside of it with my fingers – only for a moment – before I hurry inside trying to recall its being there before. Surely.

I sit by the cold stove in the kitchen in the afternoon, quaking. Is someone trying to kill me? My God.

4

Again Elaine has turned her sumptuous buttocks against me and gone to sleep dissatisfied and I lie awake with my shame and the dark around me.

Some nights as a child I crept into my parents' room and wormed my way into the bed between them and slept soundly, protected from the dark by their warm contact.

Now, I press myself against Elaine's sleeping form and cannot sleep with the knowledge that my back is exposed.

After an hour I get up and prowl about the house, investigating each room with quick flicks of light switches and satisfied grunts when everything seems to be in order. Here, the room where my mother read, here, Jamie's room where I slept as a boy, here, where my father drank his hot, milkless tea in the mornings.

I can think of nothing I've done to offend the neighbours – I'm not a dog baiter or anything – though some of them grumbled about my putting my parents into the Home, as though it was any of their business.

I keep thinking of axe murders, things I've read in the papers, horrible things.

In the living room I take out the old Scrabble box and sit with it on my knee for a while. Perhaps I'll play a game with myself . . .

5

This morning when I woke in the big chair in the living room I saw the floor littered with Scrabble tiles like broken, yellowing teeth. Straightening my stiff back I recalled the dream. I dreamt that I saw my body dissected, raggedly sectioned up and battered and crusted black with blood. The axe, the old axe with the taped hickory handle, was embedded in the trunk where once my legs had joined, right through the pelvis. My severed limbs lay about, pink, black, distorted, like stockings full of sand. My head, to one side, faced the black ceiling, teeth bared, eyes firmly shut. Horrible, but even so, peaceful enough, like a photograph. And then a boy came out of the black – it was Jamie – and picked up my head and held it like a bowling ball. Then there was light and my son opened the door and went outside into the searing suddenness of light. He walked out into the backyard and up to the chopping block in which an axe – *the* axe – was poised. I felt nothing when he split my head in two. It was a poor stroke, but effective enough. Then with half in either hand – by the hair – he slowly walked around the front of the house and then out to the road verge and began skidding the half-orbs into the paths of oncoming cars. I used to do that as a boy; skidding half pig-melons under car wheels until nothing was left but a greenish, wet pulp. Pieces of my head ricocheted from chassis to bitumen, tyre to tyre, until there was only pulp and an angry sounding of car horns.

That does it; I'm going down to the local hardware store to buy another axe. It's high time. I have thought of going to the police but it's too ludicrous; I have nothing to tell: someone has stolen my axe that used to be my father's. A new axe is what I need.

It takes a long time in the Saturday morning rush at the hardware and the axes are so expensive and many are shoddy and the sales boy who pretends to be a professional axeman tires me with his patter. Eventually I buy a Kelly; it costs me forty dollars and it bears a resemblance to my father's. Carrying it home I have the feeling that I'm holding a stage property, not a tool; there are no signs of work on it and the head is so clean and smooth and shiny it doesn't seem intended for chopping.

As I open the front gate, axe over my shoulder, my wife is waiting on the veranda with tears on her face.

'The Home called,' she says. 'It's your father...'

6

The day after the funeral I am sitting out on the front veranda in the faint yellow sun. My mother will die soon; her life's work is over and she has no reason to continue in her sluggish, crippled frame. It will not be long before her funeral, I think to myself, not long. A tall sunflower sheds its hard, black seeds near me, shaken by the weight of a bird I can't see but sense. The gate squeals on its hinges and at the end of the path stand a man and a boy.

'Yes?' I ask.

The man prompts the boy forward and I see the lad has something in a hessian bag in his arms that he is offering me. Stepping off the veranda I take it, not heeding the man's apologies and the stuttering of his son. I open the bag and see the hickory handle with its gummy black tape and nicks and burrs and I groan aloud.

'He's sorry he took it,' the man says, 'aren't you, Alan? He—'

'Wait,' I said, turning, bounding back up the veranda, through the house, out on to the back veranda where Elaine and Jamie sit talking. They look startled but I have no time to explain. I grab the shiny, new axe which is yet to be used, and race back through the house with it. Elaine calls out to me, fright in her voice.

In the front yard, the father and son still wait uneasily and they look at me with apprehension as I run towards them with the axe.

'What—' The man tries to shield his son whose mouth begins to open as I come closer.

I hold the axe out before me, my body tingling, and I hold it horizontal with the handle against the boy's heaving chest.

'Here,' I say. 'This is yours.'

Wake

Sunday He wakes and finds her gone. He has slept heavily and dully during the night. The sky is pink through the curtains. He stands with his back to the window and looks at the twisted sheets. There is a hollowness in him which he ignores. Down the street, the first-gear roar of the ute is echoing in the teeth of front fences. He goes out to meet it, watches the bellowing fishermen jump fences and spring back on to the truck. They come to his house, yelling greetings, all six of them. He waves. A thick, tanned fisherman, Tuglio, jumps the small fence and slaps a snapper on to the veranda beside him.

'Good night?'

'Not bad,' Tuglio says. 'Where you lady?'

'Bed, still,' he says.

Tuglio rattles the cast-iron railing as if to wake her, hurdles the fence and runs, laughing, back to the ute.

The snapper is pink and pinker in the morning light. He takes it by the tail and brings it inside.

Near noon, he telephones his father. He smells the tannery down the road as the sea-breeze arrives.

'Hello, Dad. She there?' His father sounds surprised and perplexed. 'No, it's OK. No, nothing. You what? OK, yes.'

He hangs up.

He fillets the fish slowly, carefully, the way his father taught him, and cooks two pieces for lunch.

Monday He wakes late. There is a small snapper on his veranda with the newspaper and the milk. There is too much milk; he shuffles things in the refrigerator to make room. He fillets the fish before he begins anything else, leaves the white flaps on the sink to firm, and sits down to his books, smelling his fingers each time he turns a page. He saturates himself with his work; he refuses to be distracted.

Mid-morning, he rings her extension number at the office; there is no answer.

In the evening, he eats dinner with his mother and father at their home. He gives his mother some snapper fillets to cook. His parents are grateful for the fish; it is expensive in the shops and his father no longer goes out in the boat. When dinner is over they sit out on the veranda in the warm night and talk. He avoids any conversation concerning her.

At about ten o'clock his father asks: 'Do you want to go for a run?'

'Where?' he asks.

'Down to the beach and back.'

'He does it every night,' says his mother with some pride.

'OK.'

For the first block, he manages to keep pace with his father, but gradually begins to drop back. His father's footsteps smack on the bitumen. He sees his father's bare back, glinting with light sweat, pull away from him, until his father slows down for him.

'You're too good for me.'

'You're damned unfit for your age. You'll be dead by the time you're forty.'

'It's not a bad age to go.'

'What would you know,' his father says.

They flash past parked cars, long, dry tresses of wild oats.

'Do you think she'll come back?' his father asks, easing.

'Yeah. Yes. I suppose.' His legs ache; his breath burns.

His father grunts and speeds up. He follows, smelling the salt of sweat and sea.

Tuesday There is no fish. In the afternoon he goes to the markets and loses himself in the fragrances of food and wood and incense and the crowd. As he leaves the markets, the sun is setting and the sky is purplish-pink, about to collapse into a tumult of thunder and warm rain. The colour suggests pain; he sprints home with a bag full of vegetables. He leaves his house and runs down to the fisherman's harbour to see the sunset. He watches the sun melt into the livid ocean and walks back in the warm rain, conscious that he has not come here just for the sunset. He disallows himself the memories.

He lags behind his father in the dark. He is tired of eating snapper. His father does not speak.

Wednesday This morning there is a big, mottled squid on the veranda. He is cheered for a moment, but when he is cleaning it in the sink he realizes that there is something wrong. He turns the squid over several times in his hands; there are three eyes. It angers him. He throws it in the garbage and goes to his books and works fitfully.

Running with his father, managing to keep pace with him most of the way, he mentions the squid.

'Seen it before,' says his father. 'Once. Cuvier, I think. Funny, eh? A mutation, I s'pose.'

He keeps abreast of his father's pumping arms.

'What did you do with it?' his father asks as they turn for home.

'Threw it out.'

'You're a wasteful bastard,' his father says sharply, pulling away until he is twenty or thirty yards ahead. They remain so spaced all the way back.

Thursday Before dawn he waits for Tuglio and the others. He intends to speak to them about the squid. He has no idea what he will say, but he is still angry. When the fishermen do not arrive, he goes inside. He eats breakfast, throws the snapper fillets out to make room for the extra milk, and begins work.

After lunch, he gets up to find a pullover; it has turned cold and it is raining. Looking in his cupboards, he realizes that her clothes are gone. She has been back while he was gone. He goes, surreptitiously, to look for her. He walks downtown, the newsagent's, the bookshop, Papa Luigi's café; nothing. Then he goes to the fishermen's harbour, between the stained vessels flexing at their moorings. He sits on the end of the jetty in the rain for a few minutes, then leaves for home, chilled.

His father is quiet in the darkness. Neither lets the other ahead. The sky thunders. They run in the gentle rain. As they turn for the return lap, his father asks him suddenly: 'Have you ever wept? Cried, I mean.'

He does not reply. Nothing more is said. Rain hisses about their feet.

Friday No fish. The neighbours are asking him about her. Is she sick? He says she is not, certain that they know and have seen her, and only ask to see his response. He rings her work extension. Another woman answers. No, she is not available at the moment, she is busy. He does not leave a message; he does not identify himself. I won't give her the pleasure, he thinks.

In the evening, he rings his parents. His mother's voice is somehow hostile.

'Your father isn't up to a run tonight. You needn't come.'
'Is he sick?'
'No.'

There are long pauses in the conversation. His mother seems uncomfortable.

'How is your work?' she asks.
'Oh, all right.'
'Yes.'
'Mum.'
'Yes?'
'She's staying there, isn't she?'
'Your father's waiting for his tea.'
He hangs up.

It rains all night. The bed, suddenly vast, does not warm.

Saturday Before dawn he hears the fishermen's trucks pass, grinding up the street. He has slept poorly, on one side of the big bed. He lies awake late into the morning, sensing the unusual heat of the day. At 10.30 he goes outside on to the veranda. It is hot in the sun; it startles him. There is a big pink snapper on the step. It is stiff and dry from the long exposure. He takes it by the unbending tail, scales rasping his palms. He leaves the milk; it has curdled in the sun.

He goes into the empty house.

Lantern stalk

It was like playing soldiers. Egg began to see it was a game they could play without shame, out here in the bush. The sergeant major called 'Parade!' from back in the clearing, and the shadows of other school cadets crumped past as he tried to secure his ground-sheet tent in the twilight. His mother had insisted he come. He was bewildered. So many pieces of equipment. Everything proceeded too fast. The sergeant major's call became a scream. Egg lifted his block-of-wood boots and fell in with the others.

Officers appeared with searing torchbeams. They were teachers in fancy dress. The sergeant major brayed: 'Atten-haargh!' Forty boys came raggedly to attention. It was the sound of a stampede. The sergeant major berated them. He was a school prefect and he played full back in the school team. Egg could smell dyed cotton and nugget and webbing and trees and earth. Stars were beginning to prick open the sky.

Captain Temby spoke. Even in the twilight Egg could see his beergut. He had felt Temby's sawn-off hockey stick on the back of his legs at PE more than once.

'Tonight, men, we're sending you on a lantern stalk.' A cheer; they liked to be called men. The sergeant major growled, 'For those of you too stupid to know what a lantern stalk is, I'll explain the aims and objectives of the exercise. You will be trucked out into the hills by the sea, and on the highest hill will be a lantern. Your task is to make it to the lantern, or inside the white circle of tape around the light, without being detected and tagged. Two men will be guarding the light. They have a fifteen-yard circle to cover. Ten officers and NCOs will be patrolling the area between you and the light. The aim is not to get seen, heard, smelt, felt or tasted. In short: not to get *caught*. At nine we will sound the trucks' horns to signal the end of the exercise. Be careful, for Chrissake.'

The darkness in the back of the truck was full of elbows and knees and the vegetable smell of sweat. Someone smoked. Next to Egg, Mukas and Roper told jokes.

Egg had found make-believe soldiering fun at first. Earlier in the year when he'd signed up there was the brand-new bag of kit: boots, uniforms, webbing, beret, and the trips to the rifle range at the edge of town where he tried to shoot cardboard men off the face of the embankment. He learned to pull apart an SLR rifle and an old Bren gun, to read maps and to use compasses. His mother said it would make a man of him, but his father looked at him sadly when he came home from parade, and didn't say a word. From his room at night he heard his parents arguing. His mother's voice was strong and rich. She spoke well. Egg's parents never got along. These days he saw little of his father who worked so hard in his office, seeing other husbands and wives. Each Saturday evening, Egg heard the chatter of his father's typewriter. The phone rang night and day. Egg's mother and her friends drank sherry and spoke well in the living room. When she was angry, his mother called his father 'Reverend Eggleston' and he left the room looking whipped and pale. She kept Egg away from 'that church'. She broiled Egg with tears. 'I should have married a man,' she said. He hardly ever saw his mother and father together.

Egg was conscientious about homework. He stayed in his room a lot where it was peaceful. In the early evenings he jogged and bits of song came to him in the rhythm of his breath. He wasn't exactly unhappy. He often thought about Stephanie Dew whom he'd caught looking at him twice in Maths. He smelt apricots in her hair when she passed him in the corridors. The proximity of her made him sad.

Some nights Egg had a dream. It was always the same: he was running up a staircase. Something terrible chased him. He could not see it or hear it but his bursting heart told him it was terrible. All along the staircase were doors padlocked against him. He hit them and sheered off them and staggered on, too scared to scream, upwards, up, twisting into the sky. Upon reaching the last step he woke. There was nothing beyond that last step, he was certain of it. Only cold space, some void to fall through forever.

'Hey, Egg, what's your plan?' Mukas asked. 'Hey, hey, Eggface!' Mukas pulled Egg's beret down over his eyes.

'Get out of it, slag-bag,' Egg said, shrugging away.

'What's your strategy? How you gonna get up to that lantern?'

'I dunno. Crawl like they said.'

'I reckon walk. Just get up and walk like you couldn't give a stiff. Reckon that's the trick.'

'Crawl, I reckon.'

'You'll never make it by nine o'clock.'

Egg shrugged in the dark. He didn't care; he was thinking about his parents. Probably, they would get divorced. He wished they could be normal. His mother was stronger than everyone else's mother. People said she wore the pants. And no one else's father was a minister.

With a whang, the tailgate of the truck swung down and someone bawled at them to get out. In the still darkness Egg heard other trucks in the distance. He got down and waited with the others by a wire fence. He smelt cow dung and wet oats. The ground oozed up wet chill. A long way off, the sea.

A light appeared small and fierce in the distance.

'All right, spread out,' the sergeant major said. 'It's a lot further than it looks. Don't let it out of your sight.'

A horn sounded, as though miles away.

'Go on, get going!'

Egg set out with Mukas and Roper, slouching along, boot-heavy. For a while there was nothing else in the night but the suggestion of crickets and the shuffle of bodies. No one spoke. They walked, hands in pockets, until a bark stopped them dead and a torch beam lanced across from the right.

'Middleton and Smythe – you're dead! Back to the truck.'

Egg fell to the ground. All around him, others did the same. He pressed into the sweet, wet earth, and he lay there listening to the others moving on. A stalk of grass poked his lip and he drew it into his mouth. For a while, he had the inclination to just go to sleep there and then, give the whole thing a miss. The whole exercise was stupid. Why the hell did his mother want him squirming up and down hills? He could be alone in his room now, or out in the streets jogging by uncurtained windows with the whole world baring itself to him.

He didn't know how long he lay there, but it was long after he stopped hearing others move past, long after he heard any movement at all. He would stick to crawling. With infinite care he began to belly-crawl to the left, clearing the way ahead before edging forward. Flank 'em, he thought vaguely. He crawled for a long time. The ground changed. In time he heard trees and began to make out their shapes against the sky. He picked his way through twigs and leaves until he rested behind a log with its smell of charcoal and ants. He was sore.

A cow bassooned softly. Egg lay on his back. The sky pressed down and it made him think that if someone knocked the chocks from the right corners, the whole lot would crash down and the world would be as it must once have been, with no margin between earth and space, no room for light or dark, plant or animal, no people. He had tried to write a class paper on the subject, but the teacher returned his opening paragraph with a suspicious glance.

Dew and cold reminded him that he had a lantern to stalk. He struck out again with a strange restlessness, sliding quickly over the even ground so that when he keeled out into nothing he wondered insanely whether he hadn't crawled off the edge of the world. He fell, filled himself with air, and had it driven from him a moment later when he hit the bottom of the washout hard enough to make white light behind his eyes.

He got up quickly and fell down again. With his head on cold sand, he lay still and waited for the sky to settle. He was calm: it wasn't the first time he'd been badly winded. As before, he told himself he would not die, that breath would return. His heart felt engorged as it did when he dreamt his dream of the spiral staircase. He was afraid.

When he had his wind back, he rose and slewed about in the washout for a moment before aiming himself at the silhouette of the bank and scrabbling up. He came upon a fence which sang as he climbed through. He was tired of playing soldiers, so he walked brazenly through the shadows of a paddock, looking for the light on the hill and someone to blunder into for the sake of getting it over with. Only, he could not find the light. Crawling, as he had been, with his head to the ground, he hadn't seen the light for some time. He couldn't even remember when or where.

Egg marched on. He whistled. Quite suddenly, a light appeared. Below him, to the left. He galloped. Where had he been? He was above the lantern. Had he gone round behind? His boots thocked through wet, dung-thick, downsloping pasture. A dog barked. He stopped. It was a farmhouse. He was stalking the wrong light. Feeling reckless, he pressed ahead anyway. A dog spattered out of the dark to greet him, to blunt itself on his shins and whimper. Egg scuffed its cold slick coat and walked with it towards the light of the house. Lamplight streamed from a paned window, illuminating the shapes of parked vehicles. Egg moved carefully between flat-tops and utilities. In the house, people were singing, and to him it sounded like an old movie. He felt his heart fill again. He crept to the window and saw faces in the burnished light of a Tilley lamp.

Big rough-faced men and women with blunt chins and black eyes stood in a semicircle by the fireplace. A bearded man in a bib and brace held a white parcel in his arms. Egg saw the chequered smiles of the people. He saw their hands. A man near the end of the semicircle warmed the back of his legs by the fire. Tears glistened on his face. Egg was dumbfounded.

The big man with the white parcel looked around at those present and then to the window. Egg ducked. The dog pasted his face with its tongue. A door opened. Egg flattened himself on the ground.

'It's cold out.' The voice of a man. 'Come in by the fire.'

Egg rolled over and looked up at the shadow.

'Come on, soldier.'

Inside there was quiet. Roots sputtered in the fireplace. Egg felt the faces coming to bear upon him. The man with the white bundle ushered him to a spot by the fire. Egg's uniform steamed. The bundle in the man's arms gave a tiny cough. A baby!

'Now,' said the man with the baby, 'we'll get on.'

Egg stole a look at the people in the room. They looked like farmers, people who knew what they thought. An old woman in a pink dressing-gown had two fluffy balls peering from between buttons. They were ducklings, he saw, and she was keeping them warm.

'What I was gunna say is that this kid is a bloody miracle. That little heart just suddenly starting to beat – that's a miracle. Tonight we claim God's promises for this baby . . . er . . . Bill, what's the name again?'

'It's,' the man with the tears cleared his throat, 'it's Sidney Robert James Maitland.'

'Like Bill said. And tonight we swear ourselves to the sacred duty of raising this kid up to hear God. That's what this is about. We love each other, we try. We look after each other in our way, and that's miracle enough in this world. And now there's one more of us. Let's just hope the poor little bleeder can remember all his name.'

Everyone laughed and the man started to pray with the baby in his arms. Egg studied the still faces in the room, wondering who they all were. It was like a secret society, a Resistance meeting. The furniture in the room was pushed back against the walls: an old sofa, a card table, treadle sewing machine. The floorboards were polished. Egg felt warm and comfortable, but his heart remained engorged.

A loaf of bread came around the semicircle, and Egg, following the others' lead, broke a piece from it and ate it. The man holding the baby took the loaf from him and put it on the mantelpiece above the fire. A ceramic mug came around in the same manner and Egg drank from it. The liquid was warm as blood and it made his mouth shrivel, his belly glow. When Egg had drunk like the others, the mug went on the mantelpiece beside the loaf.

Then Egg saw that white bundle coming around, hand to hand, and his heart thickened and he felt it rising in his chest. Each person receiving the baby touched his face, looked into his eyes, and kissed him on the forehead. As it came to him, Egg felt panic. He was certain his arms would never bear the weight. The vanilla-smelling pupa slid into his arms, heavier even than he had expected. His knees creaked. He wanted to run away. How could such a thing be borne? It was insupportable. Someone coughed good-humouredly and Egg looked up.

'Serious business, soldier,' said the man in the bib and brace.

Egg glanced around at all the expectant faces. Some of them were rutted with tears. He freed one arm, reckless, and touched the infant's cheek, noticing his own blackened hands and clogged fingernails. He looked into the child's eyes. They were the colour of the night sky. Egg kissed the cool, sweet brow, then passed the baby to the man with a weak, faint sensation fluttering in him as though it had been an ammunition box he'd been holding and not a newborn.

'Amen,' said the man.

'Amen,' said the others.

'Beer and cake, then?' asked the man, holding the child for them all to see.

'Beer and cake!' they replied with a cheer and the room was suddenly full of movement. Egg stayed by the fire, almost dry. A thin woman in a mohair jumper put a glass of beer in his hand and a wedge of rainbow cake in the other, saying: 'You're a godfather, soldier.' Her smile surprised him. He was drinking beer. No one had asked him questions. A small man with no hair on the back of his head showed him how to play the spoons. The dog whined outside. Someone fiddled with an accordion. The night seemed so real. He could do nothing but stand and watch and listen and feel the panic of wonder. The beer was sour and cold as brass. His mouth rioted when he filled it with cake. He was dizzy; it was the light-headedness of the jogger. He was more than himself. He felt deeper and wider. He felt as though he was more.

Then the room went quiet. People cocked their heads to listen. Egg put his glass down. He heard the horn far out in the night.

'That's for me,' he said, going to the door. The man with the spoons saluted him. As Egg stepped out into the dark, the fat man who had presided over the ceremony put a hand on his shoulder and pushed a lump of rainbow cake into his hands.

'See you again, soldier.'

'Where?' The man shrugged.

Egg nodded.

Moving out across the paddock, Egg looked up to see the lantern away to his left, high up, miles away, it seemed, and to him it looked like a star descended from the night sky, from that darkness in his dream at the end of the staircase where he had never yet ventured. The locked fingers of his ribcage relaxed. He was not afraid. He stuffed rainbow cake into his pockets and began to run.

Thomas Awkner floats

1

Although he had never been in an aeroplane before, Thomas Awkner was not a complete stranger to flight. His earliest memory was of the day the swing on the back veranda propelled him across the yard and into the fence. The ground rushed beneath him. Borer holes in the wooden paling became mineshafts. Impact was devastating. A loose picket pinched his earlobe and held him captive and screaming until his father could be hounded away from his incinerator behind the shed. Now, as the big jet staggered through the turbulence out over the desert, he twisted that earlobe between his fingers and sweated. He did not like to fly. His own height gave him vertigo.

Flight attendants lurched up the aisles. Drinks spilled. The FASTEN SEATBELTS sign chimed on and off. The thirty seats ahead of him were occupied by what seemed to be a delegation from the Deaf Society. These men and women wore blazers and little berets, and for most of the flight they had been engaged in an informal celebration, creating a disconcertingly visual babble. Words ruffled up by the handful and faces stretched with laughter, impatience, urgency. All Thomas Awkner could hear was the chink of glasses, but for the Deaf Society, he decided, it must have been a rowdy affair. Watching them gave him a thirst. He pushed the button for a flight attendant.

While he waited, he swabbed the sweat from his palms and smiled at the men on either side of him. It was a desperate grin, starched with fear, but it went unnoticed. From up ahead came a sharp, solitary belch. None of the partyers in the aisle seemed embarrassed for a moment.

A flight attendant came, but fear had knotted Awkner's throat so that he found it difficult to speak. The woman raised her sculptured eyebrows at him. Awkner's lips moved, but his voice seemed to be parked somewhere back down in his throat.

'Are you well?' the fat man next to him asked.

'The poor man is deaf, sir,' the flight attendant said. She began to mime eating and drinking. Thomas Awkner flinched.

The fat man scowled. 'I don't think he is. He's not wearing a blazer, or even a beret.'

'For God's sake, man,' the triangular man on Awkner's right protested, 'a man doesn't need a blazer and a beret to be deaf and dumb. He's probably freelance.'

'Rubbish,' the fat man said, 'he's listening to us now.'

'They lip-read, sir,' said the flight attendant.

'Could I have a beer, please?' Thomas Awkner managed to say at last.

'See? He talks.'

'So what?'

'Sir, honestly, it doesn't mean a thing!'

'Emu Bitter, if I could.'

The flight attendant beamed at him and went to get the

drink. Neither man spoke to him. He felt as though he had upset them terribly. He wedged himself between their anger and their outsized bodies, and thought about his two hours in Melbourne. Right across the continent, he mused, long enough to deliver a manila envelope and board another plane home.

Since he was five years old, Thomas Awkner had been running family errands, taking small boxes to strange doors, relaying single words through holes in fibro walls, passing notes to men in grey hats in windy harbourside streets. The Awkners took for granted his apparent idiocy and he did nothing, as he grew older, to unsettle their assumption for fear of losing his only measure of importance in the Awkner web. An idiot, they thought, was the best courier possible. Understanding could be a risk. So the young Thomas Awkner cultivated complete incuriosity; he ignored message or parcel and concentrated on the trip, feasting on the world outside the asbestos house with its smoke and secret talk. But the trip always ended with a return home where nothing more was expected of him. At home, therefore, he did nothing.

He was flying. His father had never flown: that fact made him feel sophisticated. His father was a memory associated with the endlessly smouldering incinerator behind the back shed. Boxes of shredded paper were often brought through the house at every hour of the night. He recalled that long, grey face with its seedy moustache and perennial white stubble. His father died ten years before. An aerosol can had exploded as he peered into the incinerator. Uncle Dubbo appeared out of nowhere to attend the cremation service.

His beer arrived. He drank it quickly and immediately his bladder demanded relief. Lurching down the aisle toward the rear of the plane, he felt as though he was swinging across a ravine on a rope bridge. The turbulence was frightening. He fought against it in the chrome cubicle but he emerged with one hot, wet trouser leg, regardless. Grabbing at coatsleeves and the occasional head of hair for support, he found his way back to his seat and wedged himself between his large fellow-travellers. The two men wrinkled their noses and glanced knowingly at one another, and Thomas Awkner was spared no shame.

All across the continent he sweated. It took time for him to realize that it wasn't only flying that had put fear into him: it was his own curiosity that frightened him. Never before had Thomas Awkner, the courier, experienced the slightest interest in the messages, the mysteries, he bore. What was in the envelope? What did it mean? Why fly across Australia to deliver it in a public place? He longed to take it out of his pocket, hold it to a window, sniff it, rattle it, but these things would draw attention. Whose attention? His new-found curiosity brought fresh fears. Could this mission be *dangerous*? He sweated.

All he could do was deliver something and come back as always, as though a rubber cord anchored him firmly to that asbestos house in the coastal suburbs. But suddenly it seemed difficult. His filtering process was breaking down. When he went back would he still be able to absent himself from the workings of the family? He had learnt that skill early on, from the year Aunt Dilly and Aunt Celia had dossed in his room with him. Their snoring, their belches and mutterings, their stockings hanging like jungle snakes and their stares across the curtain as he dressed – these things he taught himself to ignore, and fairly soon all the machinations of the Awkner family happened on the grey, outer limits of his awareness. He did not question the prolonged absences of his brother and his Uncle Dubbo. He never wondered about the huge unmarked containers their milk arrived in, or the boxes of unstamped eggs, the sudden appearance of a television set. Conspiratorial laughter broke through the asbestos walls like cricket balls, and all those years Thomas Awkner studied the discipline of inertia: he watched little, listened little, said little, did little. His schooling was not superb. He had no friends. And when, quite suddenly, the Awkners left town for Melbourne, he found himself alone with his mother.

2

The airport terminal was confusing: so many escalators and shops and purposeful people, and it was difficult to make headway, always casting looks over one's shoulder. He walked into the women's toilets, had to pay for a box of doughnuts he knocked to the floor, and was dragged from a Singapore Airlines queue and interrogated by customs officers. All he wanted was a taxi, and when he did find the taxi rank, the city of Melbourne seemed short of taxis.

After a wait in the sun, a cab eased up to the kerb beside him. He got in.

Pulling away from the rank, the driver asked him where he wanted to go.

'The gallery,' Thomas Awkner said.

'What gallery?'

'The art gallery.'

'Which one?' asked the driver, getting a good look at him in the mirror. Thomas Awkner was not a settling sight. His fine blonde hair stood up like wheat to the sun; he had not shaved; the flight had left his clothes rumpled. He stank of urine. 'Which art gallery, mate?'

'The proper one.' He was confused; he hadn't expected this.

The driver shrugged and took a punt and a left turn. 'How long you in town for?'

'Two hours.'

The driver settled lower in his seat. After all, what kind of man stays in a town for two hours? Not the kind of man you told knock-knock jokes to. He drove faster. Thomas Awkner skated about on the seat of his pants, smitten by the strangeness of the place. The buildings were half buried in trees, their lines were soft and their textures aged. It reminded him of Fremantle where he was born: houses standing shoulder to shoulder, old men walking in narrow streets. It charmed him. It flooded him with memories of walking to the wharf with his father. They lived in Fremantle to make it more convenient to visit relatives in prison. The air was full of gulls and the stench of sheep ships and harbour scum. Some days, Thomas walked with his father to the wharf where they would meet strange men and his father would whisper with them in the shadows of hawsers and derricks. The shimmer of the water's surface tantalized him. He always wanted to dive in. He begged his father to let him paddle at the little beach behind the mole, but there was never time and his father mentioned sunburn and rips and sharks.

'You'll sink like a stone,' his father said. They were the only words he remembered from his father.

The taxi stopped with such suddenness that Thomas cracked his chin on the ashtray of the seat in front. It cleared his head for a moment. He paid and got out into the disarming sunshine. He had an hour and a half left. He was to meet Uncle Dubbo here beside the dormant fountain in fifty minutes. It was hot in the sun. The sight of water running down glass attracted him to the building. He went in.

An atmosphere of sanctity was in the place. Tiny lights from heights. A brooding quiet. He decided to wait in there out of the heat until it was time to deliver. He saw his startled face in glass cabinets full of obscure artifacts; he recognized his hooked nose on a Roman bust and his doe-eyes in a Dutch oil painting. He saw pieces of himself everywhere. Normally he could not even bear to see his own reflection in the mirror.

It was thirty minutes before he saw the ceiling and when he did, the oddest sensation touched him. Stained glass – acres of it, it seemed. Fremantle. The old church. He remembered. On the way home from the wharf sometimes, he had followed his father into the old church where the sailors went, and he would be left to stand at the back near the door while his father went down towards the sanctuary to speak to men dressed in grey suits with hats in their hands. Often they would come away with little parcels which his father took out to the incinerator later in the day, but while they were speaking, Thomas was mesmerized by the scenes in stained glass at either side of the church. Every candle seemed to point towards the strange characters and their animals. On the way home, Thomas would dawdle behind his father, heavy with wonder.

In the middle of the gallery, Thomas Awkner took off his coat and lay on the carpet, looking up at the canopy of colours. Time passed beyond him as the panels of coloured light transported him back. He had forgotten wonder long ago and had replaced it with a dejected kind of bewilderment with which he armed himself to fight off the world from the slit-trench of his unmade bed. In those days of wonder, he had not been repulsed by his own image, he had not been afraid of his own height.

A man stooped and touched him on the shoulder.

'Uncle Dubbo?' If it is Uncle Dubbo, he thought, taking in the man's neatly pressed trousers and blazer and the well-organized face above them, then the plastic surgeons have done a first-class job.

'Sir, you can't lie here all day. There are vagrancy laws in the state of Victoria.'

'Oh.'

When he got up he saw that he'd left a wet patch of sweat on the carpet in the shape of a man, and by the time he had reached the door of the men's toilet people were noticing it. In the glittering hall of the toilet, Thomas Awkner splashed his face with water and looked at himself brazenly in the vast mirror. He was tall. His thin blonde hair was matted but not entirely disgraceful. His face was lean and his features thin and (perhaps, he thought, it's the heat) even vaguely elegant. The sight drilled him with that odd sensation again.

He heard a shifting sound in the cubicle behind and was suddenly afraid. He touched the manila envelope inside his shirt. He was a courier. A curious courier. Whatever it was he was carrying, he knew, it was important enough to be wanted by someone else. Perhaps everyone else. Thomas Awkner fled the toilet and walked quickly back to the entrance of the gallery, telling himself with fervour: 'I've got a mission.'

Out under the blinding sun, gelato vans had parked beneath the roadside trees. People sat around the perimeter of the fountain pool. A hot wind stirred deciduous leaves along the pavements and traffic passed, fuming. No sign of Uncle Dubbo. Twenty minutes left, yet. He wondered what he would say to him. A year had passed since he'd seen his Uncle Dubbo, and yet, in all the years through which his uncle had come and gone, in and out of his life, he had never really looked hard at him. Uncle Dubbo never engaged him in conversation. Maybe he'd put the old man through a few conversational hoops before delivery. How bad did he want this envelope? What would he do to get it? What *was* Uncle Dubbo really like? What did he *do* all these years? What about those grey ghosts, his own brothers? He could barely remember them. Maybe, he thought, a few questions might be the price of delivery, this time. Was it really an aerosol can that blew the old man's head off? What does it all mean? What's my life honestly been about, for God's sake?

Thomas took out his return ticket and turned it over. Stuffing it back in his pocket, he bought an ice cream and sat at the edge of the pool. Two small boys tugged their shirts off and made shallow dives into the water, stirring up a sediment of leaves and potato-chip bags as they skimmed along the bottom and came up gasping beneath the NO WADING sign. People clucked in disapproval. Thomas watched the boys, envious. He had put his jacket on again to cover the bulge of the envelope, and the heat was unpleasant. He watched at the boys duck-dived and came up with coins. A woman next to him, long breasted, long faced, crinkled her shopping bags and rattled her tongue.

'Decent people throw their money in there. To make wishes.'

He looked at her. Reflected light from the water was unkind to her face. He opened his mouth to speak, then closed it again. A moment later he came out with it anyway, grinning like a clergyman.

'Well, so will they when they grow old and stupid.'

She cut him with a stare and turned away. With their hands full of coin, the two boys ran across the pavement to the ice-cream vans, footsteps evaporating behind them. When they came back with dripping cones and smeared faces, Thomas Awkner was untying his shoelaces. The woman turned to stare at him. He returned her stare and without taking his eyes from hers slipped sideways into the water. She screamed, brushing drops from her dress, while Thomas Awkner struck out across the mucky pool, ice-cream in hand, to the cheers of the boys. Cool water rushed through his clothing and he felt like singing. His head cleared and he remembered his father's words. Resting at the end of the pool, he watched the boys finish their ice creams and churn across to where he floated in the shade of the gallery. Behind them he saw the sports jacket and feather-duster moustache of Uncle Dubbo. Thomas lay on his back. He spouted like a whale. He had not been seen. Uncle Dubbo had black eyes. His fists opened and closed as though he might lash out with them at any moment. Thomas recalled suffocating clouds of cigarette smoke, toneless instructions, a plate thrown.

He patted the soggy lump in his shirt. The boys dived around him and he felt the rumour of a laugh in him. The strange city rang in his ears: sound and sight limitless. Uncle Dubbo paced, fists in his pockets. Thomas Awkner floated.

Wilderness

For five days and five nights the man and woman had been in the wilderness. The last food stand of karri was hours behind on the bluish hills against the sky. In the mist of early morning the scrub and rock of the coastal hills were the same steel-grey, and each footfall resounded, steady and unambiguous. They could not see the ocean but they knew it was less than an hour away. They had not come to see it. Marsupial droppings flattened moistened underfoot. Their packs had not yet begun to weigh heavily upon them; it was early.

He waited for her to catch up. It was unnecessary but it gave him an illusion of leadership. She read her bird identification book as she walked. Even as he watched she stumbled on a stump and fell to one knee, driven to the ground by the weight of her pack. He waited. She turned the page. Clouds skated in from the south. They were at the end of the continent. After the ocean there was only the half world of the Antarctic.

'You shouldn't read while you walk,' he said.

'It's a skill worth having,' she murmured.

'Well don't break a leg acquiring it. I couldn't carry you out.'

'It's just that we should be able to name all the birds we see. It makes seeing them worthwhile,' she said. 'Common sense.'

'I wouldn't have thought so. While you've got your beak in that book you're not even seeing the birds.'

The walked another twenty minutes. The bush, as the light grew, turned blue and was unbroken on every side, unmarked until the paler blue of the sky capped it at the uneven horizon. On the spine of a long, granite-studded ridge they took compass readings and, looking eastwards down the valley, saw – for only a moment – a metallic glint. When they moved their heads it flashed. The man took a reading from it. She thought: Metal? This is wilderness. God, don't let it be a car. The idea itself was a desecration to her. Neither spoke. As they cut down the valley through the thick strew of boulders on the slope, the bush rang in their ears. They lost sight of the flash immediately. For five days there had been wilderness, no person, no sign of a person, not even a footprint. They moved down in the direction of the flash.

The valley was thick with head-high trees and dense, scrubby undergrowth around lozenges of granite in the cracks of which grew nests of pigface. The walking became difficult.

Bush-bashing, he thought; just what we need.

They stopped before a thick wall of growth that appeared impenetrable. Resting, packs cast aside, they were beset with a strange feeling: they had left their planned route, broken the timetable. In all their walks this was the first time. They had digressed.

'Maybe it was something in the rock that glittered,' the woman said, fingering her book.

'Like fool's gold.' He sighed and opened his canteen. He saw seams of dirt in the earliest lines of her face. 'We said we'd walk six hours. We've exhausted ourselves.'

'This isn't as good as the Bibulman walk,' she murmured. 'Or others.'

'There's a gazetted stream a kilometre east.'

'Funny, isn't it,' she said, 'how we always walk to water.'

'Common sense, I'd have thought.'

She looked at him and sucked her furry teeth. It was the same answer she'd have given to such an uncharacteristically whimsical statement. After all, she thought, chastising herself, who but a mad person would walk out away from water?

Hoisting themselves into motion again, they skirted the dense growth for several minutes until they came to a space, a tunnel in the tangled and matted foliage, that looked as though it had been made by animals. The man bent down to it. On his belly, there was enough room for him to move forward with his pack. The woman stood behind, watching his rump disappear, thinking: We've gone off course for a flash in the bush. It amazed her. A ludicrous thing to do, quite out of character. She got on to her belly and followed the scent of his sweaty buttocks.

The undercut in the bush widened until the man and the woman could crawl abreast of one another across the tortured roots and between the stems and wizened trunks of the vegetation. Marsupial droppings and the shadows of birds coloured the detritus. The woman and the man came out into the light together and helped each other to their feet. What they saw caused them to cry out simultaneously. Fifty yards further downhill in the clearing stood the aluminium frame of a dwelling.

'My God,' she said.

He shook his head. Within the frame hung a wooden door. A petrol-powered cement mixer stood to one side and with it, a shovel, a trowel and a screed. An aluminium window as big as a man leant against the near side of the frame.

'This is *wilderness*,' he said.

'Impossible,' she whispered. All around the cleared site, the scrub was the same: knotted, olive-drab and seven feet high. The lower side was confused and thickened by boulders and some taller trees. The woman pointed out the stumps and dead brush trodden flat on the ground all about. The clearing was man-made, someone had slashed the vegetation flat.

The man went to the door and opened it. It was eerie to step over the threshold and into the square of ground enclosed by that cage of metal. He walked through the space where the exterior wall would be.

'Yes,' he muttered, 'impossible.'

'And illegal,' she added in disgust.

'How could people carry all this gear in here? The nearest vehicle track is eight kilometres away.'

In all the bushwalking they had done over the years they had never come upon anything as inexplicable as this. They had done a lot of bushwalking. In their five years of marriage they had become connoisseurs of national parks and wilderness trails. The passion had not visited them by chance. After their first married year when it became evident that beyond their shared enthusiasm for courting, they had almost nothing in common (they read little and disliked team sports, and though minor, their musical interests were irreconcilable), they drafted a list of hobbies a husband and wife could share, drank a bottle of wine over which they had bickered bitterly, and arrived at two final possibilities: the Gestalt Club and bushwalking. Being afraid of religion and expense, they chose bushwalking. They bought their equipment, did their reading, and after the first year found they had a taste for it. Being teachers, they had a good number of lengthy holidays and their walks became more adventurous. Between walks they bored their schoolteacher friends with their hobby. In time, they were not invited to dinners and parties. They stayed at home and planned new walks. To the fresh crackle of survey maps, they filled their evenings with sensible conjecture and reminiscence. They upgraded their equipment. They became connoisseurs.

The husband lowered his pack to the ground and sat. 'I want to find out about this,' he said, wiping his brow with the sleeve of his shirt.

'Me too,' the wife murmured. 'It doesn't make sense.'

Later they retreated to the hedge-like vegetation and crawled just inside its shade and its tintinnabulation of cicadas. He took water from his pack and she the Hexamine stove from hers, and they made a billy of tea. They rested in the shelter drinking tea until the late afternoon, each secretly annoyed that they were allowing this strange discovery to distort their itinerary.

'It makes no sense,' she kept saying. 'You don't build houses in a gazetted wilderness.'

'And if you do, you don't build a kilometre away from the nearest water, and you don't build a house with those materials. And hack your own clearing. Only a lunatic would.'

They settled in to wait.

Night fell. They unrolled their duck-down sleeping bags,

and after a meal of reconstituted rice and vegetables, slept lightly, listening to the rustlings of tiny animals in the invaded space beneath the scrub. The husband woke in the darkness before dawn with an aching bladder. He slid from his sleeping bag and crawled out into the clearing and was only beginning to relieve himself when he heard a metallic rattle somewhere out of his vision. He cut himself short, cursing inwardly, and slipped back under cover. The sound repeated itself. He woke his wife. They listened, peering out into the dark. A jarring thud; it was closer, but the bush, they knew, was deceptive. The thud again, and the rattle. Excitement prickled in the man and the woman. They strained until they thought they could hear each other's pulse. Then the bush down across the clearing began to vibrate and they heard scrapings which continued for several minutes. She was the first to see the outline of the figure that emerged and the shape that so slowly followed it. She touched her husband's arm and whispered: 'There.'

'A bloody wheelbarrow,' he whispered.

The figure was hunched and moved with the hesitancy and weakness of an old man. His coarse breathing was quite audible. With the convergence of dawn upon them the man and the woman began to see with less difficulty. For some time the man stood over the barrow, grunting and cursing. Then he straightened, puffing, each breath a bellow, and kicked the barrow over. A bag of cement thudded to the ground. A few tools chattered down beside it. Then the man himself fell. He did not move. For some time the wife and husband remained silent and motionless, watching, but there was no movement. They stared. The woman shifted her gaze to see her husband in the corner of her eye and she felt something turn in her belly. She thought: He looks sort of handsome when something gets his whole attention. Like a child, all intent. She had never experienced this distracted, disturbing sensation before; she was admiring him. At her side, he was thinking: This is a madman we're watching. We're losing walk time.

From beneath their shady hollow the wife and husband felt the day's heat creeping overhead, taking hold of the wilderness, claiming back the glittering jewels of dew, and as the morning came on and on, the man in the clearing by the houseframe and the spilled barrow did not move. They assumed he was sleeping; there was no sign even of his being alive.

But the man lying beside his battered barrow was breathing, albeit in narrow snatches. He had walked eight kilometres in the night, pushing his barrowful of cement, and he intended to repeat the trip as soon as it was dark. Inside his exhausted body he was dreaming. In his dream there was only the ultramarine sound of the wilderness sky and the sound of his heart labouring and he felt a profound satisfaction as he was raised up into Heaven. Flies dozed on the domes of his eyelids. Not even they sensed the intruders on the perimeter of the clearing he had hewn in the wilderness.

By noon the husband and wife had become quite uncomfortable in their nook, changing prone positions carefully, front, side, back. They hardly dared crawl back whence they had come for fear of alerting the man in the clearing. They did not consider revealing themselves and greeting him as if by accident. He looked unpredictable. Besides, their curiosity had grown and their resolve had hardened with every uncomfortable hour. They communicated by facial expressions and occasionally a whisper. As they waited and endured, an exciting sense of complicity took hold of them. In that cramped lair there was a novel intimacy. It was unnerving. He fed her tiny bits of chocolate, taking infinite care with the foil so as not to make a sound. She took it on her tongue silently as a communicant, tasting the salt on his fingers, holding one fingertip captive between her lips until his thumb buttoned her nose back and he smiled.

There was none of this at home. Their home was a place of business. No time, no gestures, no thoughts wasted. There were careers to attend to, unlikeable children to teach, Remedials to suffer, Exceptionals in whose glory to bask. Evenings were begun with sociable complaints about the staff and equipment of their respective schools. Then papers were marked, lessons prepared, and before bed a little mild gossip was exchanged. It was not a frivolous life. Even in their walking they were not frivolous. They mapped out their journey, they walked from A to B to C without unnecessary deviation or lingering at any point, and they gained their satisfaction from telling themselves, and the few who would listen, that they had *done* this walk and *done* that wilderness trial. Walking was a means to an end. They did not believe in things that were ends in themselves.

Somewhere inside her, the woman, taking chocolate from her husband, felt the impulse to explain their behaviour as a means of passing time. But the feeling was hollow. Instead, another sensation, a springing of nerves in her pelvis, in her chest, her feet, had come upon her, and though part of her demanded to stifle it, she drew it upon herself deliciously, licking her husband's fingers, pinching the tips in her teeth, holding her tongue out to him before he had another piece of chocolate to hand. And she noticed his quickened breathing, the reckless way he opened a second bar, the way he thrust his finger into her mouth and moved it across her teeth and around her gums.

Without pausing from this intensifying ritual, the woman unbuttoned her heavy cotton shirt and saw her husband's teeth meet and his lips move as she revealed her small, damp breasts, and from that moment, as she pushed him back on to the uneven ground and felt his breath in her mouth and his belt buckle hard against her belly and her waistband stretch and the vegetation against her shoulders and in her hair like frenzied fingers, the man prostrate in the clearing was forgotten. She heard her husband's breathing in her ear. She tasted chocolate and sweat and felt him reaching inside her without fear, without reserve, without precision. He bore her down on him. It was passion. It made no sense.

In his dream, the man in the clearing rose out and away from the curve of the earth, the compromising sounds of nature, the expressionless and unseeing eyes of those ugly little boys he lived with five days of the human week, the spiritless books that crowded his bedroom and his reference lists, the bloodless words and meaningless syllables he taught – all of them fell behind as his exhausted body and his burning soul lifted free and rose and rose. He felt himself yodelling and hooting, tumbling upwards to that clean, well-lit, sensible and airy room in which he would be received.

When he woke to find himself earthbound, he let out a groan and watched the dusk sky passing overhead. His legs, his feet, his back, his head ached. He thought: dark . . . time to go again . . . time to work. In one ragged movement he got to his feet, righted the empty barrow and began his agonized shuffle back across the clearing to the scrub. Down on his hands and knees, he dragged the barrow through and under the clot of vegetation. Twigs and trunks tore at his hands and his hair, snagging on the awkward shape of the barrow, until he was through and into the thinner open scrub outside where he could wheel the barrow ahead of him, jolting it over rocks and stumps downhill. It was eight kilometres to the Land Rover.

Lying in a stupor, feeling the sweat dry on their skins and the guilt creep into them, the wife and husband heard the man go. His groan of disappointment had made them flinch because they had forgotten him. They followed the progress of his shuffle and the creak of the barrow wheel across the clearing, and then listened to him bashing through the scrub until nothing more was audible.

'That's bloody odd,' the husband said, startled by the sound of his own voice after so long a silence. It was the longest period without speaking he could remember.

'Is it safe?' she asked, noting the lack of intimacy in his voice.

'I suppose so.'

She scrambled out to stretch and to urinate and brush herself clean and button herself up. Stars had appeared in the sky and a chip of moon was illumined just above the uneven horizon.

'We need water,' he said, tasting the residue of chocolate on his tongue.

'Why is he doing this, do you think?'

'He's either a criminal or a lunatic.'

'And he's coming back, I'll bet.'

They had wandered cautiously down the clearing to where the bag of cement lay near the door of the skeleton house. In the moonlight they could plainly see the weals his boot heels had left in the ground.

'He's no econut, that's for sure. Look at the materials, the way he's hacked the bush.'

'Still curious?'

He nodded. 'What about water, then?'

'We'll get some and bring it back. He's got hours to cover. We could find water pretty quickly, if we're lucky. Enough for tonight and some of tomorrow.'

He shrugged, agreeing. But he was still uneasy about the broken itinerary.

They took the waterbottles and the billy and with a map and a compass, made their way east, the same way the man had gone. It was difficult and dangerous work in the dark. There was no time for small talk.

It was late in the night when the man came willing his body up the incline towards the clot of scrub. Two bags shifted and shook in the barrow before him, one of builders' sand, the other of bluemetal, and he held them in his gaze as though they were sacks of precious stones. Sweat slicked him, and his lungs felt blistered and broken. He didn't even bother to confuse his movements or to stop and start again at odd times or to swap trails or lie and listen any more because he knew deep in his rawness of exhaustion that any deviation, any pause, any confusion would be final, that if he lost sight of that tangible bar that connected him, pointed him to the scrub clot on the slope – he couldn't tell if the white bar was light or pain – then it would be over. All his life, it seemed, he had been working towards this. Energy burned white in him even now, but his body was failing him;

it did not understand that all things were possible. God help, God help me, he thought. Fifty weekends, a hundred trips, had not been enough. He had taken sick leave, holidays, even a day-trip after which he fell asleep in front of a class of thirty-eight teenagers. But still the structure went up slowly, awkwardly, fell down and was put up again as he read from how-to manuals and held screws in his teeth and felt the righteous anointing of sweat on his body. At first the work had been frenzied and the results quick to be seen by the eye. He cleared the circle in the scrub in four days: his machete flew, blinded him with its sunflashes, moved of its own accord. But the structure, the carting under secrecy and peril of darkness, the logistical odds . . . Men, he knew, had dragged riverboats through jungles and over mountain ranges, built pyramids, towers, walls that were impossible but for the will. It would go up because he had will, and because it was the most logical thing in the world.

From their position under the nest of scrub at the perimeter of the clearing, the man and woman heard him coming. They had washed and drunk at the tiny creek at the bottom of the valley, finding it by ear in the end. They had returned several hours before, and were roused from their light sleep by the noises. The woman, washed of this afternoon's stickiness, felt a renewed excitement at the sound of his approach. It was as if a great secret was about to be revealed.

The husband moved back slightly further into the foliage. There was no wind, no bird sounds, only the wispy, close movements of nocturnal animals and the distant creak and rattle of the wheelbarrow. The man was already wondering how he was going to make this story credible to the others in the staffroom. He never listened to a story that was not credible, and he would certainly not tell one. He was proud to be a teacher, a man of reason, disseminator of rational learning. This afternoon's incident in the bush had unnerved him. He tried to organize the past twenty-four hours in his mind, but the creak of the barrow wheel, even louder, distracted and confounded him. He gave up and listened to the madman's pained respiration.

Down at the lower end of the clearing, the undergrowth rattled and snapped and screeched against the metal of the barrow. Each expiration was a distinct groan: 'Ugh, ugh, ugh.' It was like the sound of a labouring locomotive. The moonlight caught first the slick of sweat on his back, and then the metal sides of the barrow, and the man and woman, close to the ground in their hiding place, saw at once how fiercely his limbs trembled. His shoulders jerked, his legs danced beneath him. His mechanical breathing underwent a change as the laden barrow tipped suddenly on its side and then he was down on the ground, beating feebly at the earth, weeping. The sound became more and more animal, more shocking in the quiet of the wilderness. His body sent out a vibrato distress call like that of a wounded ram. They listened for a few minutes until it became obvious that he would not get up and the bleating would not stop.

Everything in him hurt. Everything. His soul ached like a tourniqueted limb. His body jangled him, smothered him, refused to move, refused to stop, refused. Stars closed in upon him, shining drops of sweat. He tasted salt. Remember, he thought, you are salt. He wedged his tongue between his teeth to stop them battering. He felt himself looking outside his body to the night above, as though he had scratched two holes in the lid of his own coffin. And that strange mewling sound in his head that disgusted him slightly would not cease. Beneath the sound, something in him said: 'I am trying, I am trying,' in a mellow, patient tone. Shivers rolled over him, end to end, faster, until there was no calm between swells. The black bowl of sky glittered benevolently.

I have to mix cement, he thought. I have to build, to measure, to carry, to make. I have to establish here to wait. I have to be here. I have to be here. Then his body stopped for a moment and he heard in the calm the sound of his heart punching, working, building, carrying, and his body relaxed as his soul's voice said, 'Then I'm here?' and there was only the bleating sound far away and the mild heat in his throat.

He was not surprised to see the two angels hovering above him, pinned against the velvet bowl of black sky. Their faces were clean and well fed. They were decent-looking angels; he was not disappointed. There was concern and innocence in their decent-looking faces and he was touched. Warm hands on his chest. A woman angel with black hair that fell over him, a warm ear to his swampy breast. Then they were looking at one another with worried angel faces. Although their lips moved, he could not hear their words for the mewling in his ear. This is it, he thought, this is truly it.

Their decision was reluctant but inevitable. There was only one reasonable path of action: the man had to be carried out of the wilderness. He was gravely ill. The husband and wife were grateful in a way that the situation and common sense itself left them with so few options. There was no argument; it took only a few moments. She stayed with the trembling, wailing, sick man while her husband went up to get their packs. His eyes were open, following her in an odd, unalert way, and sweat continued to appear on his bare chest and on his blackened, unshaven cheeks. She prised open one of his fists and saw nests of white blisters in his palm. Crazy, she thought; this is absolutely crazy. His jeans were tight and heavy with sweat. From one of his pockets she extracted a leather wallet, fat with money and an identity photo she could not see clearly in the moonlight. The money was a surprise to her. She wondered if perhaps he had stolen it.

At her side again, her husband, panting slightly, began sorting the contents of the packs.

'We'll have to go absolutely light,' he said. 'Anything superfluous has to go. Anything that'll weigh us down that we don't need in order to get him out.'

The spare changes of clothing spilled on to the floor. A pair of carnival-coloured underpants made him wince momentarily before they were obscured by the roll of the tent, the billy, the birdwatching manual, spare maps, excess food, and tiny items that looked anonymous and useless in the moonlight.

'Can we do it?' she asked. She watched him stuff the essentials into one pack.

'We'll have to. Besides, can a man do all this?' he said, with a gesture taking in the clearing and the partially built dwelling.

The woman pursed her lips and looked at the sick madman whose cries had begun to subside. 'Who knows?' she murmured. 'Does he look successful to you?'

The man zipped and sealed the pack and turned to the prostrate body. 'Let's get him into the bag.'

After they dragged his heavy boots off and shunted him feet-first into the sleeping bag and had him zipped up and hooded, they began the arduous task of lifting him into the barrow. It took ten minutes. His body bent and sagged awkwardly. The nylon exterior of the bag slipped between their fingers. His body was like a bag half full of stones. And all the time, as they heaved and dropped and cursed and staggered, his eyes passed from one to the other of them, infuriating them with a lack of expression. When he was in, feet out between the handles, buttocks in the hollow of the tray, head out over the front lip of the barrow, they wedged him tight with the spare clothing and rested for a moment.

He saw their earnest faces moving above, and the sky still benevolent over their shoulders as he felt himself levitating and moving away, the earth turbulent under his back. He wondered if his mother would miss him. She, even this past year, had never suspected, never known where he had been coming every weekend, never even understood or detected his sudden and vast dissatisfaction with his life, with her, with his useless job. Never, as they sat at dinner with the ABC news gently whispering to them across the room, had she suspected that he raged inside. But he ate his chops or his meatloaf and the cabbage that tasted like wet newsprint without letting go his secrets. Yes, he thought, she'll miss the company at the table. But she'll get in a boarder. And I forgive her. I forgive it all. These thoughts saddened him. His mother had, after all, given him a home, a room of his own, the chair at the end of the table after his father left them. But he had never known much feeling for her. The day he saw her in X-ray vision he knew why: she was an empty vessel. The white light of her soul, that radioactive ball, was deep in her large intestine, lodged firm, unable to be shunted through her bowels. He understood then.

Now he felt himself floating downhill, saw the pale biscuit moon running along the tops of the faraway trees, and felt himself at a so-long-awaited peace. But it puzzled him that things proceeded so slowly. He had imagined death and ascent into Heaven as more or less instantaneous.

The night seemed determined to last for ever. There was nothing to mark its passage but the endless punctuation of jolts, curses, near-spills and the occasional soft bleats from the invalid in the wheelbarrow. The husband and wife did not speak; there was no room in their lungs. The husband felt the gradual lengthening of his arms and sagging of his burning shoulders as he held fast to the handles, forbidding himself to let go. The woman at the front expected at any moment to have her heels fall away. Walking by turns backwards and sideways, she struck rocks and stumps on the tenderest parts of her feet. She sensed the track. She guessed. She could rarely see where the barrow bade her walk.

This is not impossible, she thought, catching a glimpse of the long cocoon in the barrow and the wild-eyed face of her husband and the featureless shadow of the bush all about. Her husband's beard glittered with sweat each time the moonlight touched it. His breathing was mechanical, hurtful to hear. She found herself avoiding the sight of him. In his fatigue he looked as mad as the man they were carrying.

Every few minutes, after each passage of near-spills and slips, the husband found himself thinking: This can't happen, people can't do this, people don't even imagine this. But not for one moment did he hesitate. Even when they stopped to rest a moment and taste the PVC-tainted water from the canteen, there was no doubt in any part of him that he would continue.

The invalid settled back inside the coffin of himself, feeling nothing but slight puzzlement. In an effort to orient himself, he went back to the start, that lunch hour twelve months ago in the staff room when he saw the ragged noticeboard on the wall opposite become a window. It frightened him. His coffee went cold as he watched. There was bush, just bush and sky through that window, the kind of bush he had never entered before. It was lonely, untouched, risky-looking bush and it gave him an inflated feeling in his chest. When the siren sounded the end of the lunch hour, the bush and the window were gone and there was only the scabby pin-up board and the everpresent haze of cigarette smoke. Then in the first class after, while chalking up the current facts on the Russian revolution, he saw his thirty-six students lose their heads. He stopped chalking. Their hands continued to copy down his scrawl, their torsos squirmed, shins were still kicked; he saw a note being passed, but for a full minute there was not one child with a head. He turned, shaken, back to the blackboard. He sneaked a glance. They had their heads on and they were giggling at him.

It was that evening when he saw his mother's skeleton inside her. His chops actually became live coals. The ABC newsreader's jaw swung like a garden gate. He went to bed early. Every evening that week he went to bed early. That weekend, he decided to drive out of the city to the hills to think. I'm having a nervous breakdown, he thought driving up. I'm off the edge. But the moment he got out of the car a few miles off the main road overlooking a valley and a series of uncleared ridges, his body ticked like a geiger counter. Bush. He experienced the same sensation as that first day in the staff room. His blood went mad. He began to walk. He half galloped down a ravine to where pools of water and reeds and shady trees were all about, huddling in secretively. And it was there that he heard the voice coming up out of the ground.

'Go into the wilderness and wait,' it said, and the logic of it made him nauseous with excitement and apprehension. He had no doubts as to who had spoken.

All in a rush he bought Forestry maps, tourist maps, bushwalking glossies, visited the state library, drove hundreds of kilometres on weekends to find a wilderness. I'll have to build a house, he thought, I'll need a house to wait in. He began to hike and search, feeling his whole being jangle like an alarm bell as he stood on isolated crags where nothing human was visible, where the sky seemed close enough to whisper to, until he found a place that sent his blood ricocheting about in him enough to tell him *here, begin*. A white cord of light or heat rolled out before him and he stumbled in and along it until an impenetrable clump of shrivelled trees came into his vision and he saw that nothing was impossible, that all things could be done and had been done.

Here, he thought, I'll wait here. But first I have to build a house. Not even God would make a man wait out here without a roof over his head.

Every night for a year he dreamed foreign dreams in strange languages. The last few weeks, a phrase coiled through him like a loop-tape in the darkness. *Ich kann nicht anders . . .*

And now, as he saw the moon rise like an aura above the angel's head, he understood, was content, and he glided, weightless.

For a moment, the husband had the gut-sinking feeling that they were lost. The moon, behind them all along, now seemed diffuse on the horizon ahead. He called a halt. The woman, afraid to lie down for fear of never getting up again, slumped across the cocoon in the barrow, her sweat running down past her ears and into her eyes. From his pocket the husband took the flat, tiny compass and was surprised to see that he could read it without the light of the torch. East. They were still heading east. They were not off course at all. He peered at the pale light in the distance. East, he thought. East. Light. He glanced back over his shoulder to see the faded moon. East. It was the sun. He pulled a sleeve back and saw that it was five-twenty.

'Dawn,' he said. His voice sounded close and alien in the bush.

'Far?' she whispered, not looking up. She could see the barrow wheel with its tread full of little stones and burrs.

'No,' he wheezed.

But it was no comfort to them. They were appalled at the thought of willing themselves to move again. They knew such a thing could not be done. Ahead of them the earth curved upwards to a point, a ridge against which the eastern sky had begun to blanch.

A minute later, stone by stone, bush by bush, they were climbing it, the woman backwards, pulling, digging in with her raw heels, her husband hard behind with the ends of the handles almost piercing his palms as he pushed and steadied and made ground barely off his knees. Birds had begun to blur by. Their hesitant songs were lost on the man and woman who heard only the blood in their ears and the infinitely slow creak-creak of the wheel's revolution. They had forgotten the man in the barrow. Since his bleating had ceased hours before, there was only his impossible weight to remind them of his presence, and even that, after a time, became an anonymous, abstract thing that only their bodies sensed.

Once or twice during the night, the woman had thought

of the warm, sensible staff room at her school: the lively, decorous chatter, the tobacco smoke, the yarns, the certainty of it all, but now such things did not exist for her. There was only the stone-by-stone impossible certainty that she was making ground. Her husband saw the mask of her face. It had begun to remind him of the mummified monster he saw in a film as a child. The image had terrified him and his father had laughed coming out of the cinema. His laugh had sounded so confident, so matter-of-fact, and as he grew he came to remember his unreasonable fear with disdain. But he felt it again now when his wife's tortured face came into his vision, stronger with each step as the light grew on the crest of the ridge and the crest itself became close enough to seem attainable. He heard his breaths become sobs. He bent and pushed and heard the wheel creak and turn.

Through the holes in his body, the man in the barrow saw the light coming and heard the sounds of birds stirring in the scrub all about. The steady labour of his heart was still with him, racing a little as mind and soul reacted to the intensified sensations of ascent. Excitement coursed through his tiny, warm core.

The moment they reached the razor spine of the ridge and took the fresh yellow sun in their surprised faces, the man and the woman lost their grip on the barrow. It tipped their passenger into a nest of pigface. They gazed like animals at the Land Rover.

'It's impossible,' the woman said.

'No,' murmured the man in the sleeping bag, hearing the final blow of his heart and the comforting silence that succeeded it. He felt himself slipping, curving, lifting away, rising up through the orifices of his body with a silent hiss that sent his warm core out and away into the impossible, colourless light. He did not look back to the figures embracing on the ridge with his body shrouded beside them; there was no time and no need.

Neighbours

When they first moved in, the young couple were wary of the neighbourhood. The street was full of European migrants. It made the newly-weds feel like sojourners in a foreign land. Next door on the left lived a Macedonian family. On the right, a widower from Poland.

The newly-weds' house was small, but its high ceilings and paned windows gave it the feel of an elegant cottage. From his study window, the young man could see out over the rooftops and used-car yards the Moreton Bay figs in the park where they walked their dog. The neighbours seemed cautious about the dog, a docile, moulting collie.

The young man and woman had lived all their lives in the expansive outer suburbs where good neighbours were seldom seen and never heard. The sounds of spitting and washing and daybreak watering came as a shock. The Macedonian family shouted, ranted, screamed. It took six months for the newcomers to comprehend the fact that their neighbours were not murdering each other, merely talking. The old Polish man spent most of his day hammering nails into wood only to pull them out again. His yard was stacked with salvaged lumber. He added to it, but he did not build with it.

Relations were uncomfortable for many months. The Macedonians raised eyebrows at the late hour at which the newcomers rose in the mornings. The young man sensed their disapproval at his staying home to write his thesis while his wife worked. He watched in disgust as the little boy next door urinated in the street. He once saw him spraying the cat from the back step. The child's head was shaved regularly, he assumed, in order to make his hair grow thick. The little boy stood at the fence with only his cobalt eyes showing; it made the young man nervous.

In the autumn, the young couple cleared rubbish from their backyard and turned and manured the soil under the open and measured gaze of the neighbours. They planted leeks, onions, cabbage, Brussels sprouts and broad beans and this caused the neighbours to come to the fence and offer advice about spacing, hilling, mulching. The young man resented the interference, but he took careful note of what was said. His wife was bold enough to run a hand over the child's stubble and the big woman with black eyes and butcher's arms gave her a bagful of garlic cloves to plant.

Not long after, the young man and woman built a henhouse. The neighbours watched it fall down. The Polish widower slid through the fence uninvited and rebuilt it for them. They could not understand a word he said.

As autumn merged into winter and the vermilion sunsets were followed by sudden, dark dusks touched with the smell of woodsmoke and the sound of roosters crowing day's end, the young couple found themselves smiling back at the neighbours. They offered heads of cabbage and took gifts of grappa and firewood. The young man worked steadily at his thesis on the development of the twentieth-century novel. He cooked dinners for his wife and listened to her stories of eccentric patients and hospital incompetence. In the street they no longer walked with their eyes lowered. They felt superior and proud when their parents came to visit and to cast shocked glances across the fence.

In the winter they kept ducks, big, silent muscovies that stood about in the rain growing fat. In the spring the Macedonian family showed them how to slaughter and pluck and to dress. They all sat around on blocks and upturned buckets and told barely understood stories – the men butchering, the women plucking, as was demanded. In the haze of down and steam and fractured dialogue, the young man and woman felt intoxicated. The cat toyed with severed heads. The child pulled the cat's tail. The newcomers found themselves shouting.

But they had not planned on a pregnancy. It stunned them to be made parents so early. Their friends did not have children until several years after being married – if at all. The young woman arranged for maternity leave. The young man ploughed on with his thesis on the twentieth-century novel.

The Polish widower began to build. In the late spring dawns, he sank posts and poured cement and began to use his wood. The young couple turned in their bed, cursed him behind his back. The young husband, at times, suspected that the widower was deliberately antagonizing them. The young wife threw up in the mornings. Hay fever began to wear him down.

Before too long the young couple realized that the whole neighbourhood knew of the pregnancy. People smiled tirelessly at them. The man in the deli gave her small presents of chocolates and him packets of cigarettes that he stored at home, not being a smoker. In the summer, Italian women began to offer names. Greek women stopped the young woman in the street, pulled her skirt up and felt her belly, telling her it was bound to be a boy. By late summer the woman next door had knitted the baby a suit, complete with booties and beanie. The young woman felt flattered, claustrophobic, grateful, peeved.

By late summer, the Polish widower next door had almost finished his two-car garage. The young man could not believe that a man without a car would do such a thing, and one evening as he was considering making a complaint about the noise, the Polish man came over with barrowfuls of woodscraps for their fire.

Labour came abruptly. The young man abandoned the twentieth-century novel for the telephone. His wife began to black the stove. The midwife came and helped her finish the job while he ran about making statements that sounded like queries. His wife hoisted her belly about the house, supervising his movements. Going outside for more wood, he saw, in the last light of the day, the faces at each fence. He counted twelve faces. The Macedonian family waved and called out what sounded like their best wishes.

As the night deepened, the young woman dozed between contractions, sometimes walking, sometimes shouting. She had a hot bath and began to eat ice and demand liverwurst. Her belly rose, uterus flexing downward. Her sweat sparkled, the gossamer highlit by movement and firelight. The night grew older. The midwife crooned. The young man rubbed his wife's back, fed her ice and rubbed her lips with oil.

And then came the pushing. He caressed and stared and tried not to shout. The floor trembled as the young woman bore down in a squat. He felt the power of her, the sophistication of her. She strained. Her face mottled. She kept at it, push after push, assaulting some unseen barrier, until suddenly it was smashed and she was through. It took his wind away to see the look on the baby's face as it was suddenly passed up to the breast. It had one eye on him. It found the nipple. It trailed cord and vernix smears and its mother's own sweat. She gasped and covered the tiny buttocks with a hand. A boy, she said. For a second, the child lost the nipple and began to cry. The young man heard shouting outside. He went to the back door. On the Macedonian side of the fence, a small queue of bleary faces looked up, cheering, and the young man began to weep. The twentieth-century novel had not prepared him for this.

A measure of eloquence

Along the clay cliff-edge the sagging old radio wires cut the wind with a yawl. The young man and woman saw that down on the point in the grove of trees were two tents and a caravan.

'Jerra told us this place was deserted,' said Ann, looking down at the campfires.

Philip paused, hand on the door of the hut, and looked down to the beach and the trails of footprints that looked so tiny from up there. He said nothing, there was nothing he could say. The exultancy had receded and disquiet had come upon them, the kind of restless anxiety which visits people in the wake of momentous actions. They had been married for two days.

Before last night in the motel room, they had never slept together in a bed. Now, in this rough hut on the cliff, they found themselves straightening blankets too hastily, tucking the corners with awkward, terribly casual movements. The big iron bed consumed most of the space in the single room. Ann slotted a cassette into the tape recorder and the music helped diffuse some tension. The interior of the hut, with its patchwork of tin and asbestos and pine packing-cases, seemed more benign in the light of the Tilley lamp. There was a deal table, two chairs, a bench with a bucket set into it, a few shelves fastened to each wall, and an oblong strip of linoleum on the floor. The hut belonged to the father of a friend. Their friend had lived here for a year after a nervous breakdown. There was no sign of his occupancy except for a few books on the shelf by the bed: *The Coral Island*, *Under the Volcano*, *Reach For the Sky*, *The Sun Also Rises*. Philip pulled down *The Coral Island*. The dust made him sneeze. Ann turned from the window and smiled.

'Did you read it as a boy?'

'No,' he said.

'I did.'

'You were never a boy, though,' he said, trying to shrug the heaviness from him.

'Sometimes I was.'

'This marriage could be embarrassing, then.'

'Don't worry,' she said with a grin. 'I won't tell.'

He put the book back on the rough shelf and sat on the bed. It sagged in the middle like a hammock. Rain started to fall and the tin roof chattered.

'You want some tea, something to eat before bed?' he asked.

'No,' she said. She drew the salt-stiff curtain.

Ann woke to the sound of the camera shutter. Pink light made the blankets and the linoleum floor and the bedstead blush. Philip, elbows on the windowsill, focused the zoom lens. She saw the dawn in his hair, on his bare shoulders, on his right cheek.

'The sea,' he said.

'The what?'

'The sea. The sea.' The camera plunked. He wound on.

'What about it?' She bunched the pillow beneath her neck.

'Nothing. Just . . . the sea.'

'Now you sound like Jerra. You don't even like the sea. You hate fishing. You even hate people telling stories about shipwrecks. You don't even go to the beach in summer.'

'Yes I do,' he said. He was conscious of his untanned nakedness.

The day came out of the sea at them. Birds hovered on the updraughts before the cliffs. The gas stove hissed. The smell of eggs overpowered the dust and the mildew and the last scent of sex on their bodies.

Neither mentioned last night as they wandered along the beach with the cliffs and the hut and the old radio wires high above. Ann held her folio hard against her hip to keep the wind from having it. Philip's camera swung from his neck like a grotesque charm. Rain had pummelled the roof in the dark last night, drowning their cries. In those first moments after waking, Ann had a feeling of having flown. Philip recalled her boyish shoulders against his teeth, and the taste of talcum. Both, even now as they kicked up sand and saw the distorted shadows of gulls on the beach ahead, had the sensation of having come somewhere, the night traveller's disorientation upon arriving, at dawn, at a town which bears no recognizable features, no signs, no immediate relation to the last stop.

A mile up that endless beach they stopped and Ann sat to sketch. She sketched poorly and they both knew it, though it remained a tacit secret. Philip watched her work from a distance, close to the shore where the sea ate at the sand.

'How does it feel to be married?' he called.

She did not answer; it seemed as though she had not heard. How does it feel? she was thinking. It feels like waking up on your twenty-first birthday and realizing that there's no change, that you don't feel an ounce older. That's how it feels. So why ask me? You know how it feels, it's written all over you.

Through the zoom lens Philip saw that she was not drawing at all; she was thinking. He snapped that sad expression on her lips and the thread of hair in the corner of her mouth, and wound the film on with a sigh. We shouldn't have come here, he thought.

On the cliffs at dusk, just at the soft edge where run-off wore steep veins in the clay, they found a pair of brogues, toes pointed out towards the sea. In each shoe was a sock. They were still warm. Footprints embossed the clay surface near the brink. Behind them, the sun was far gone in the hills. It took Ann a moment to realize that she was alone. She saw Philip running along the brow of the cliff towards the safe path to the beach. She did not call him; her throat was swollen with dread. She stood at the edge peering over. She could see nothing; even the beach and the vegetation at the bottom was dissolving rapidly into night.

When finally he joined her again, wheezing and wet with exertion, his embrace told her that he had found nothing.

'I don't understand,' she said.

'No.'

'It might be a joke.'

'Yes,' he murmured, 'a joke.'

They could not find the shoes again in the darkness. They went back to the hut where they had left the lantern burning.

That night, a storm bore down and the little hut quivered in the wind. They picked at their food and drank too much wine and lay in the big hammocky bed, listening, unable to shed the sensation that enclosed them. The wine had fuelled their sadness and apprehension. They touched each other; their nakedness seemed frivolous; their bodies felt ludicrous.

'I can't,' he said. 'I'm sorry . . . I can't.'

She turned her head into his chest in the dark.

'No, neither can I.'

'We shouldn't have come here,' Philip said. 'It was a mistake, it was my fault.'

'We were both there when he offered it to us.'

'It just doesn't feel right. Like sleeping in a morgue, or on a deathbed.'

'You're exaggerating,' she murmured. 'Anyway, it should be the opposite. It's where he came to get well. It's a haven, a refuge.' But all the time she was thinking of Jerra's tears, his tossing and twisting, his great sadness in this single room. And the shoes, the shoes would not leave her mind.

'You know, if we were fishermen, fisherpersons,' he said with a shallow cheerfulness, as pieces of dust were forced from the cracks in the wall by the force of the wind, 'we'd be up planning for the morning's fishing, making lines and putting hooks and things on them, telling tall tales, not getting depressed. We'd be—'

'But we're not,' Ann said without expression, and immediately he regretted having sounded so desperately light-hearted. The wind in the falling old radio wires that had once linked boats and crews to their families ashore gave out a cry that made him think of boats lost at sea, families grieving – even the out-of-work shearers over on the point with their campfires and their taffy-haired children and the piles of beer bottles by their tents. And he thought of those shoes and the warm socks inside and wondered whether it was a sick joke or whether he would find a broken body on the beach in the light of dawn.

An hour before dawn Ann woke, weeping. She saw only darkness and felt Philip close beside her.

'What's the matter?' he asked, half-conscious.

'I had a dream,' she said. All her limbs restrained a sob.

Philip sat up. The air was sharp. It was beginning to rain again.

'I dreamt that this hut fell off the cliff and we were killed. Someone found us with our feet cut off. We were dead, all bloody, without clothes, and there were people all around.'

He put his hand to her cheek, felt her wet face in the dark. 'Well, we're not dead.'

After a long silence she said: 'Have you ever seen a dead person?'

'No.'

'I have. When I was thirteen my aunt died and before the funeral started my parents made me go in and look at her. She was . . . like something out of a sideshow. They made me.'

'One of my friends,' Philip said quickly, 'father was killed when we were in high school. He was a road worker. A carload of kids ran him down. My old man was the local copper. He had to take my friend to identify the body. His mother was in hospital having her appendix out or something. Dad brought him home to our place after the morgue and he was weeping like a baby. Dad left us in my room. I put my arm around him and then we were both really embarrassed so I took it away. I think I was expected to say something, but I'm not like my old man. I don't have those kinds of things to say. Fine bloke, my Dad. I always wanted to be him. I still want to be like him, I suppose.'

'What? Dead?'

He smiled after a moment, thinking her comment a desperate joke, but in the half-light he saw her face in her hands and he was wounded. 'What's wrong?'

'I don't want to die. I don't want you to die.'

'People die,' he said hopelessly.

She gave him a traitorous look. Now they could see the rain on the window, long cords of it torn out of plumb by the wind. They slept and woke spasmodically, watched the weather through the window, heard the linoleum flap and the wires wail until late in the morning. They spoke little.

When they rose, they ate thick squares of bread daubed with honey and drank the Irish Breakfast tea they had brought specially. The other treats and specialities they had brought for this week were still on the shelves: Spanish olives, ambrosia cheese, chocolate, pecans, kiwi fruit, things they had gloated over on their way south that seemed so unappealing now.

'Let's see if we can walk to the end of the beach,' he said. He had honey on his chin.

'Which way? Towards the point?'

'The other way.'

'It's miles.'

'Why not?'

She shrugged. 'I had thought of reading.' She pointed to the book at the foot of the bed.

'Don't bother. I've read it. About that legless pilot—'

'Douglas Bader.'

'Well I thought you'd rather walk than read about artificial limbs.' Then he laughed. 'Has this got anything to do with your dream?'

She scraped the honey from his chin with her index finger. 'Let's go then.'

It took them ninety minutes to come to the end of the seemingly infinite white curve of the beach. There was a headland, some rocks, and a half-exposed reef. They climbed along the rocks to the reef and saw nests of cockles along the waterline. Philip lowered himself feet first to where the water surged in, and filled with cockles the bag they had brought for shells.

'I suppose you can eat them,' he said as they walked back in the afternoon sun.

'Jerra says they're like mussels or oysters.'

'Poor ol' Jerra.'

Half-way back they noticed two figures moving towards them on the beach. It annoyed them and made them walk faster to reach the path up the cliff and regain their seclusion. But it was further than they thought and they soon tired. Before long, they saw the figures were the old couple they had seen arriving with their caravan on the first day.

'Oh God,' Ann muttered when she realized they were going to meet.

The two couples met. They exchanged pleasantries and the old man asked them what they had in the cloth bag. Philip told him.

'Cockles,' the old man said. 'Lovely things. Where'd you get 'em?' They told him. He seemed disappointed. 'Give my right arm for a feed of cockles.'

His wife agreed. She was a small woman with her white hair braided and pinned to the side of her head.

'You want some?' Philip offered, annoyed.

'Oh, no.'

'It's a long walk,' Ann said, 'and it's pretty precarious down on the rocks.'

'Oh, Jim couldn't do anything like—'

The old man seemed to cut her off with his grimace.

'Here, take half of these,' Philip said, pouring cockles into the old man's doffed hat. Ann looked as surprised as the old man. Philip felt a secret pleasure.

'Jim has a marvellous recipe for them,' the small woman said. 'We'll trade you.'

'Yes, yes,' said the old man. 'We'll trade you. And I'll give you a cup of Sauterne to marinate them in.'

Twenty minutes later the four of them were sitting in the caravan. The old man poured Philip a beer and the women lemonade.

'Lovely set-up you have,' Ann said. She felt trapped in this over-furnished mobile home.

'Oh, you'll have one like it, someday,' the small old woman said. 'Always nice to start small.' She then went on to talk about her five daughters and their weddings. Philip observed her husband across the table. The old man had a tremulous air about him, little hair, gold rimmed spectacles, a good suntan, and moist eyes. Philip wondered whether he was an alcoholic.

'Of course,' the woman continued, 'Jim would have liked a son. Fathers like to have sons. But he had his work.' She told Philip and Ann how her husband had taught at the technical school for thirty-five years, and of his recent retirement and the sale of their house, her husband all the time moving his spectacles about on his tanned nose as if graciously allowing himself to be spoken about. 'He got tired of those boys. They had no home discipline.'

'But some of them could really work with wood,' he said. He was assuming control of his story. 'And I liked them, tried to get them on side for thirty-five years. I just didn't have the tongue for it. Not a good enough tradesman to be a carpenter, and not good enough talker to be a teacher. Wanted most of all to be a teacher.'

'But you *were* a teacher, dear,' his wife said with a worried glance.

'But not a teacher with his class in the palm of his hand. All I needed was that little measure of . . . eloquence.'

'His last class put in together to buy him a gold-plated drill-bit.'

'Their little joke.' He smiled thinly.

Philip looked at his watch. It was late. The cockles in his bag had begun to smell.

'Married long, dears?' the old woman asked as they made to leave.

'Two days,' Ann said, drinking the last of her lemonade with some effort.

'Well, if you could have some of *our* forty years, you'd be a happy couple, I'm sure.'

'Yes.'

*

Half-way along the cliffs where the radio wires drooped like laden clotheslines, Philip laughed suddenly and swung the bag of cockles up high.

'The old bastard didn't even give us the Sauterne.'

There was a coldness in the hut that night. The delicacies remained untouched, the cockles went rank on the bench, the wind blew and the lamp hissed. They ate bread and honey and put their elbows up on the deal table, unable to say much. They found it difficult to even allow their eyes to meet. In bed, Philip thought of his friend, the one whose illness had shocked him so. As she tried to read the opening of *Under the Volcano*, Ann thought of the old woman's words: 'You'll have one like it, someday,' with a turning in her belly.

Ann whimpered in her sleep. Philip was awake. Surf cracked down on the beach. The wires kept up their mournful sound.

Towards noon the next day Ann and Philip sat in the sun on the broad beach, and sketched and took photographs.

'What are you drawing?' he asked.

'The cliffs. What are you taking pictures of?'

'You drawing the cliffs.'

'Here come our mates,' she said.

Philip turned the zoom down along the beach, focused and groaned. 'And they're bringing a bag. He's gonna get some cockles, I'll bet. Not to be outdone.'

'You shouldn't have put them in his hat.'

'He wanted them. Hang on . . .'

'What?'

'Hang on . . .' Philip got to his feet. 'Something's wrong. The old man's down.'

'But what's wrong?'

Philip saw the woman moving frantically about the prostrate figure. 'Oh, God, we better help.'

They ran, folio flapping, camera chest-beating, and the sand broke their gait and made them stumble. The old woman was now flailing the air with her hands, hat fallen to the sand beside the head of her husband. She began to shout, then scream.

As he leant over the old man, the swinging lens of the camera caught Philip on the nose and he was blinded. Ann put her head to the man's chest and heard respiration. The woman cried: 'His heart, his old heart!'

They hoisted him on to Philip's back and tied his wrists together with his belt and threw his arms over Philip's head. For a few moments Philip felt the old man's breath in his ear. He could barely see. His nose bled. Fifty yards away, the path up the cliff began. Words, talking noise, plans, advice, regrets, they were all mashed in his ear with the sound of his own exertion. Near the top, where the footing was firmer and the noise of the wind in the wires could be heard, Philip felt a hot wet flush down the small of his back, in the waistband of his jeans and down the back of his legs.

Ann did not drive as fast as she could have. No one had conceded the old man's death yet, even though his body, sprawled across the back seat, head in the old woman's lap, was quite lifeless. She saw Philip's white face with its congealed blood smears. He looked out at the road. It was an hour before a word was spoken. The town limits were visible. Then the old woman spoke.

'Jim loved his cockles,' she said composedly. 'Loved them.'

Ann, watching in the rear-view mirror, asked: 'Did you know his heart was bad?'

'Oh yes, dear, only I didn't know *how* bad. He didn't enjoy teaching those boys, I'm sure. No, his heart was bad. I should have guessed it was giving him funny turns the other night when he went for a walk before dark and came back without his shoes. He was all confused, said he didn't know where they were. He went straight to bed. I heard him crying in the night – it must have been the pain, poor love. Well, we had a good life, dears.' She began to weep.

Philip's mouth was open slightly. Ann had noticed it was the way he slept. She seemed to be driving faster, the curves seemed more centrifugal. Ann cleared her throat. The sound made Philip flinch. Their eyes met. It was only a moment. Then they were inside the town.

The oppressed

for Loi Hong Quan

They are like children sitting in the market-place and calling to one another.
  'We piped to you and you did not dance; we wailed and you did not weep.'

Luke vii, 32

1

We are hugging. Our arms and faces and palms touch. Skins brush contrasts across one another. Their eyes glitter in their tall, pale bodies. They are Australian. I am still Chinese. We laugh exultantly. It has been months since we met. They used to visit me at the migrant hostel. But I have not come alone: by my side, Hoa is silent, half afraid of the strange boisterousness of Mary and Simon. They tug me and punch me on the back, though they become subdued when they notice Hoa and her stillness.

'You're back, mate,' says Simon who is a shaggy-haired

youth. He is younger than me, friendly, and impatient, it seems, to be friendlier. 'Quoi, you're back!'

Mary slips an arm around his waist as she often does, with her weight on one foot. She is sensitive, I feel; she wants to know things, to feel things. These are young people, and I, so little their senior, feel like an old man with them. And yet, what do I know that I would have them experience? Her narrow, pleasant face beaming, Mary asks many questions at once, almost in a single breath. There is a smell of roses in this park with its crusty statues of horses and men poised, rising and rushing forwards, clamouring silent. And browning roses.

'Yes, I am back.'

Their faces smile until they seem they may split like mangoes.

'It's great,' Mary says. I call them 'mate' and they laugh as we stroll in the sweet space between rosebeds. We are quiet for a moment; even the traffic is subdued. Mary smiles at Hoa, uncertain, but friendly. Hoa is unused to their ways and remains silent. She feels like an intruder, I am sure, but my relationship with these people is difficult to explain. They invited me into their home. They helped me. How can I explain such a thing? She folds her hands neatly over her cheap cotton dress. Her figure is minutely fine compared with the motherly thighs and hips of Mary. Their bodies seem to have thickened during these months, whilst mine has strengthened and hardened. They tell me so, and seem ashamed of their softness.

'Who's your friend, Quoi?' Mary asks.

I introduce Hoa, embarrassed at my neglect. They say hello in unison and Hoa nods politely. They are noticing her silence and I can feel them wondering. Silence worries them.

Those long reeking, wallowing nights we learned silence, huddling on the aft deck of the stolen boat watching lights pass us spectrally on the water, that water which yields more than fish and weed, throwing bloated things upon the beaches, that water which knocked fists of wavelets against the boat's hull, beckoning, taunting us with the men and women it still withheld . . .

As we walk down William Street towards the art gallery, I tell them of Broome and the other towns they have yet to see. It is very like home, I say, explaining the climate and the palms and the tides, and describing the humid, sultry nights drinking beer with the noisy Aboriginals who frighten us, but smile often and whitely in the dark. Some Europeans drink with us, call us Charlie, speak rudely to the Aboriginals. Beautiful, lonely nights sipping draughts of prickly-cold beer with froth boiling over the lip of the glass. Saigon beer, I say, has not been so good for years. Simon says he though we drank rice wine. He is joking, I am sure. Both he and Mary seem disturbed when I say Russian beer is no match for American beer. I feel sure Simon wishes to reply, but he refrains from comment.

'Where did you meet Hoa?' Mary asks, avoiding more talk on beer.

Dismissed from my job as deckhand without warning, I sat by the post office watching the waves bracing the rugged piles of the jetty as a new boat berthed, off-loading tired men who came up to collect their mail. In my hands I clutched two letters, one from my company who regretted this and that, and the other from Simon and Mary who joked about a string of illegal pearls I should bring back to use as checkers to renovate the battered set we idylled over by the river on summer evenings when we ate freshly netted prawns. It was hot and I clenched the paper between my fingers, for the first time without a reservoir of resolve, only apprehension. People speaking in the post office ...

I begin to tell Simon and Mary the parts that are not so tedious to tell.

The people at the post office were asking me did I want a job. I walked down to the jetty with them, four Eastern European men with difficult accents. A deckhand died at sea, they said, and they seemed dazed. Perhaps they too knew death, but not at sea as I did. It was something new to me. I noticed these men were speaking to me as though I was stupid. This would be a hard job, I was sure. A girl's face appeared for a moment near a hatch. She was also Chinese. My spirits rose. She did not smile ...

'Many Vietnamese working up there?' Simon asks. He forgets what I have told them of our origin. Does he do this on purpose? I tell him of the Chinese, Filipinos, Malaysians and others. No one else could allow themselves to be treated so poorly, except the Aboriginals who no longer seem to bother. Few need money as badly as us. Fewer know what Australian money is worth in our country.

I speak of the advantages of the black market and how I send money home through its revaluing channels to my parents and family in Saigon. Simon and Mary speak in gently disapproving tones. I cannot explain. There is too much for them to know.

As I mounted the gangplank, the girl's head appeared once more and I stared and lost my footing. My belongings bobbing sulkily about, I swam to the jetty, with the crew laughing down at me . . .

Hoa's shoulder brushes against me. Is she glad that these people are my friends? More than once have I thought they would make formidable enemies, so irrepressible is their idealism and goodwill. Hoa is frightened. She does not know how they will react. Her mouth is tight.

'Rough seas?' asks Simon, perhaps he is testing me.

'Nothing is too rough when there is somewhere to go,' I say with a smile. Simon nods soberly. They react this way when I mention the refugee boat. I feel they mention it to remind themselves. Sometimes they are angry and tearful about it, but more often sober and quiet.

We go into a dirty café which smells of bacon and coarse antiseptic, the sort of place Americans eat in. I am confused. Simon and Mary cannot afford to buy food. This is why we are going to the gallery which costs nothing. We sit at a slippery Laminex table with a chromed napkin-dispenser and a cracked glass sugar bowl. Simon puts the dispenser against the wall to make it like Australian toilet paper. We laugh, not really embarrassed. My brother, who designs American bathrooms, would laugh loud if he were with us.

Four egg and bacon burgers come, the sort we ate in the American places in Saigon. It was fashionable for students then. Hoa is gripping my hand. This will be hard for her. Mary and Simon seem not to notice as she spills lettuce and tomato into her lap, eyes down, humiliated. She has not yet learned to eat without her front teeth. I am embarrassed for them. People are staring, some nudging and making unquiet fun. I am embarrassed for Hoa. And perhaps myself. And my people.

She only ever told me once, late at night when most of the crew were resting and in Chinese in case they weren't. How the Thais dragged her across the deck by her legs and tied them apart with all the other people sobbing and looking away. How she had heard them beating the young men, tearing the instruments from the boat, smashing, urinating, threatening, leering as she waited mutely, too frightened to speak until she saw things which made her cry out, and she tasted the brass end of the rifle butt in her mouth, the oily, bloody taste, and the fragments and singing nerves she could not spit out. I could not know it as she did, but I had things of my own.

Some I have told to these, my innocent friends. I say nothing of Hoa's boat. They have guessed and Mary is crying.

The night I spoke of the Gulf of Thailand, Simon, too, cried; ashamed, he said. Even the Thais will not fish there, now. Their nets are invariably snagged by sunken vessels and often break under the strain of the bodies dredged up. Was Simon ashamed of mankind, or ashamed of crying?

2

Massive as walls, the paintings lean down upon us, clotted oils glistening as if still wet. I watch the 'cybernetic structure' whose photocells react to my presence, my shadow, my height. It beeps and blurts sounds, audibly reacting to me. Can it tell what I am thinking? It is a marvellous thing.

Mary and Simon steer us down long rows of pictures to a small collection of watercolours. There, says Simon. The watercolours are of men and women – peasants – working in rice paddies. They form a progression. Dread plummeting through me, I realize that these are of the war. Helicopters, candy-bars, the rickety skeleton of a live child, huts aflame. Old miseries. Hoa and I walk away, leaving Simon and Mary peering carefully at each frame, murmuring to each other in serious, indignant tones.

Puzzled, they join us at the display model of the new Congress Hall the government is building. 'Parliament House'. The model is beautiful, so pure, precise in its engineering. I feel the formulae in my mind, the slide rule hingeing against the heel of my palm, and for a moment I am resentful of such things as dirty pearling boats. The symmetry and wholeness of the structure are not apparent to Simon and Mary who pass sarcastic comments.

'Such technology,' I say. 'Marvellous.'

'Bloody marvellous,' says Simon, straining to be polite.

'You have made great advances. Like the Americans.'

They nod, and I am uncertain about the cause of their sudden ill-feeling.

'Bloody America,' Mary whispers.

On the boat with the crew sleeping around me, my hands sore from the shells and the salty cuts, I thought, not about the starless nights huddled on the deck of the other boat, but felt the old formulae in my head reeling outwards, ready to unfold themselves on paper, to do my work for me. I longed to write them into the stiff, brief postcards to Mary and Simon, but they would not understand. In any case, the formulae are different here, they told me at the Institute of

Technology. Not even Hoa would understand the formulae. She has had little education. It is easier, sometimes, without.

3

Christmas Eve. On the way to a party in Mary's old car, we speak of small things, avoiding the subject of the water-colours we saw yesterday. The exhibition was called 'The Oppressed'. Mary and Simon want to discuss it with me.

'Hoa is at the dentist,' I say. I miss her tonight.

'On Christmas Eve?'

'He is Chinese. A favour.'

We become quiet.

'Those pictures,' Simon says. 'Yesterday, those pictures – I thought you'd like them, Quoi.'

I shake my head.

'But it's about cruelty, destruction, oppression.'

'Yes.'

'But you're been there,' says Mary.

'And do not wish to return. Such things are for those who have not been there.'

These people are concerned about politics, but only of a sort. They think in fiery, innocent terms – in principles. But politics – it is how much food and who will die. We have grown up without time to wield these principles, only a numbness.

I had never lived in a bamboo hut and worn no shoes until the Area Camp. My father, a taxi driver, saved for our education over many years, before the Americans, even. Saigon had no rice paddies where we lived . . .

Simon is trying to distract my attention from a slogan on a bus shelter which almost glows in the dark. I wish they would not worry.

'Bastards,' said Mary, driving faster.

On the back lawn we sit drinking good beer, eating the grapes, watermelon, cheese, apricots and biscuits that Mary's friends bring around. I have read nothing on Christmas, and it has not been explained to me. No one mentions it. The beer is good and for a while we talk quietly between ourselves, joking about the seeds Simon is spitting into the garden. They are trying to protect me.

'Have you ever had food like this before?' a wriggling curly-haired girl asks, holding a stick of English cheese under my nose. I answer politely, telling her I have. She calls to a friend. Simon and Mary are ill at ease.

'Hey, come and meet this Vietnamese bloke!'

'He's Chinese,' Simon says with a measure of authority. I cannot help but smile.

The drinking is heavy, many people are dancing to music I cannot understand. American music. Some serious young people are talking around me.

'Who were the worst?' asks one. 'The Yanks or the French?'

Before I can answer another speaks over me.

'Was the corruption in Saigon—'

'Ho Chi Minh City,' interrupts the other.

'Bullshit!'

'What do you do?'

I tell them my qualifications and those of my eldest brother. I tell them my father drives a taxi and how he bribed an official to ignore my absence temporarily.

'Poor bastard's a victim.'

'American product.'

They speak about me as if I am not present.

'Shut up!' Simon is shouting. 'Go bite your watermelons or something.'

'Geez, Simon,' someone calls, 'the proletariat cries out.'

They all laugh. Simon and Mary gather their things and we leave, climbing over the bodies in the garden and the asbestos fence. They are apologizing for their friends as we get into the car.

'Bloody idiots,' hisses Mary, looking helplessly at Simon.

'We're sorry, Quoi,' he says.

Both are confused and embarrassed.

'It was good tucker,' I say, a word from the lugger. It catches them by surprise and they smile, and Mary leans over and kisses me on the forehead.

'They wish me to be a peasant,' I say.

'Yes,' says Simon. 'I suppose it would be easier for us, too.'

4

Tonight I must tell them.

The lights move on the river, rippling like long tapering silk worms that dance in the night. Prawns are soft and still warm from the boiling pot we have cooked them in. Vinegar runs down our chins. Mary has her feet in the water where the little bodies of gobbleguts and smelt lie discarded from our net. I run my fingers over the mesh. The piles of the jetty across from us smell of barnacles and slime. Odours I remember well.

'She's a nice girl, Quoi,' says Mary. 'I hope you're very happy.'

'Yeah,' Simon smiles. 'Good luck.'

From my pocket I take the tiny medicine bottle which has been hidden in so many places, and shake out the pearls. These are what I have collected from the bad shells, imperfect greyish-white pearls, small enough to be hidden in an ear or under a fingernail. The skipper would have beaten me, had he found out.

I show them the big one I have chosen for the ring for Hoa and they marvel at its beauty. It is not perfect, but it is surely beautiful.

'And this is for you,' I say shyly, uncertain of how they will react. The two pearls are faulty, oblong specimens with lines in their skins like scars. Simon and Mary hug me and say thank you. I am grateful, because I know they do not agree with pearls.

'Why, Quoi?' they both ask.

'Because I am going to Brisbane. Hoa's brother has been found there. She must see him before we marry, and there . . . is no money for a return fare.'

'Going? Again?' Mary looks hurt.

'We could get some money together for you,' says Simon.

'No, you cannot,' I say, truthfully.

'What about your Uni course?'

'It cannot be helped.'

We sit awhile, the light flickering in our faces, and I observe the limestone monument behind us set with a metal plaque. The limestone thing is indecipherable. I wonder if they notice it? Mary, crying, hugs me. Simon is turning the pearls over meditatively in his palm.

'They're probably not worth anything, commercially,' he says.

'No,' I admit. I am ashamed.

'A peasant's gift?' Mary asks.

I smile. I will miss these strange people.

The woman at the well

The tired horses shuffled in the dust, burying their heads in the buckets the soldier had drawn. The creak of the rope made them prick their ears, half alert. The well was old, the stones worn from animals and women.

Heavy blowflies knocked against his brow as he grunted, carrying the heavy buckets. The horses also grunted, half submerged, almost satisfied but for the wet rope that bound them. The well jutted out of the smooth, packed dirt of the deserted market-place, and the buildings around the square were full of soldiers as young and old as he. Shouts drifted from the shade. A two-up game was spilling on to the street, a nodding mass of curses and thudding coins.

It was a strange place, but the men, like all soldiers, brought their country with them. They fought and swore and slept and waited. The liberating forces called this resting. Women in the area were as scarce as in any other pock-marked town on the peninsula. They stayed indoors; too many things had happened.

Returning to the edge of the well with an empty bucket in each hand, the soldier noticed a shawled woman walking, bucket on her head, towards him. He lowered the rope again, feeling under his palm the smooth stone.

Although he did not hear her footfalls, he knew when she was behind him. Turning, he saw that she was quite young – scarcely out of adolescence – but there were lines in her face.

The woman stood, hands limp by her sides, and stared at him. He busied himself with his buckets in the dirt around the well. His arms were hairy and streaked with sweat, his shirt prickling with moisture. She watched him.

'Will you draw me some water?'

He swallowed, his mouth dry, and croaked.

'Ah-er, sure, miss.' He wound slowly, searching for something to say. 'It's a bonzer day, eh?'

She didn't seem to hear. He didn't feel like saying anything else. The bucket came to the surface, brimming with clean desert water which forced the sun into his face. The two-up game was rowdier, with the laughter of winners and the grunts of those on the lose.

'Do you have money?' Her English was perfect. The question startled him; she seemed to be speaking to someone else. Perhaps she was mistaking him for another man.

'Er, why do you ask, miss?'

Covered in a sprinkling of fine dust, the black shawl over her head was holed, and there were callouses on her feet.

'Do you have anything?'

'Pardon?' Sunlight danced in the creases of his face. He squinted at her. 'Listen, I haven't got anything you'd want.'

'Have you money?'

'. . . Yeah.'

'Will you trade?'

'In what exactly?' He grew cautious.

She put a hand on his arm. His body contracted. He was quiet for a moment. The horses drank and shuffled. There was peace here. But her hand was on his arm and his breath came out with a sigh.

'What the hell; here today, gone tommorrer. Where?'

Turning from him, she walked slowly across the square towards one of the crusted, flat buildings. With the sun on the back of his neck, the soldier loped along behind.

She stopped in the shade of what looked to him like a shop or an office, then disappeared into the entrance. Coming to the step, he peered inside, hesitant. He saw nothing in the musty darkness, heard nothing. Her face appeared; she took his hand, her palm cool against the damp heat of his.

For a few seconds the contrast in light left him blind. Led through the front room, he could see the forms of a desk and an empty bookcase. The desk was bare, edges burnt. Papers crackled under his feet. The woman padded and he clumped across the floorboards, following her into an equally dingy room that smelt of ash and sweat and urine. There was a small window high on the wall; the ceiling was black from smoke and flies. On the floor lay a large pallet, stolen from the barracks, he supposed. There were a few boxes in one corner, and a wooden chair covered in cigarette burns and graffiti.

Hands in his pockets, he stood as the woman began to undress by the pallet.

'How much, love?' he croaked, throat tighter.

'Two pounds.'

Still standing, he watched her as she lay on the gritty mattress, naked, resigned, absent. Her breasts were small, her ribs like an ugly corset beneath her skin, her belly scarred and limp. He unbuttoned his shirt, and as he peeled it from his back he heard a shuffling sound. Standing still, with his hand cocked to one side, he waited and heard it again. Then a baby wailed.

'Where's it coming from?'

The woman stayed stretched feebly on the floor. Her eyes were expressionless. The cry continued as he went over to the boxes in the corner.

'Gawd, who's this, then?'

A small head poked from a rag in the smallest of the boxes. Its eyes oozed yellow. Shaking his head, the soldier turned to the woman.

'Forget it, blossom. Here, take a quid. Buy Mohommed here something to eat.' He gave her a pound note, moist with sweat. He showed her his open wallet.

'See these? That's my kids and my wife.'

She nodded again.

'The littlun'll be two soon.'

She stared.

'I'd better get back to the nags. I'll probably be in for it already.'

The sun burst into his eyes as he strode out across the square to the well. No one had noticed his absence. The two-up game was nearing a climax of anger and laughter as he drew a bucketful of water and splashed his face and arms. Refreshed, he turned to the stomping horses and noticed the woman's bucket at his feet. He filled it then stretched his back. He saw the black robe at the doorway across the square. Chuckling, he returned to the horses. She was coming to thank him, he thought.

An insect hum crept into the air, but his mind was on other things as he checked hoofs and mouths. The woman, now halfway across the square, looked up and then fell flat as a shadow. The blur of the plane hurtled overhead, the

Turkish pilot beetle-like in his goggles and yellow scarf. The two-up game continued, a few of the less engrossed gamblers scuttling to safety, and the horses stirred.

The soldier turned. A bullet pierced his left arm, throwing him sideways to his knees. It was then that he heard the cicada sound of the machine-gun, and felt another blow in the side, just above his pelvis, and the third seemed to open his chest inwards. The horses thrashed against the ropes, falling over each other with wounds in their legs and bellies. One lay broken backed, crimson ribbons gouting down its belly. In their fear, the others trampled the beast, staggering and snorting.

On the earth near the well, the soldier lay spreadeagled, bleeding into the dust. The sound of the aircraft faded and the horses calmed a little, still disturbed by the presence of their dead.

At his side, the woman. Her eyes were empty, her mouth tight. Pinned to the dust, he breathed loud and spoke.

'There's ten quid in my wallet . . . top pocket. Keep it.'

The woman moved closer, to hear him better, he thought. She was reaching into the bloodied pocket above his heart.

'But . . . keep the pictures, the wife and kiddies . . . promise.'

She paused as he spoke, and when his words faded and his eyes were as empty as her own, she pulled out the wallet, red with blood and blue with the ink of his burst fountain-pen. Opening the leather, she took out the ten pounds, wet and torn. The bullet had passed through money, photos, papers. She noted the name embossed on the inner flap: Pte. W. Williams. Stuffing the money into her robe, she closed the warm wallet and dropped it into the depths of the well.

Turning again to Bill Williams whose blood had disappeared into the dust, she stepped over his splayed figure and picked up her bucket. It was holed and empty, so she left it by the well and walked back to the dark entrance across the square.

Scission

1

It is four o'clock. He paces through ribbons of glass, stepping hard on his heels to feel the shift and snap. As he stares at the walls with their dainty pictures of women, he inserts a magazine, secures it in the weapon with his palm. He feels the rifle's dark weight and observes the plaited sinews locking in his forearms.

He sits on the piano stool and surveys her room. In one corner there is a vase of peacock feathers on a small table. He notes carefully the fine spray of colours. The feathers ease up out of the mouth of the vase like soft words. Everywhere, inflated armchairs, animal rugs, knotted, baked pieces of clay. He is a stranger in this flat.

Light through the shattered window is soft. A breeze brings in the dry grass smell of late afternoon.

There is another smell, though he is puzzled because it is also a quality of light. Hers.

He lifts the lid of the piano gently because he is afraid of its dark smoothness. With his thumb he depresses the last key but one, and then, the last. It is like pushing white teeth. To him it makes the word:

and the last, lowest, darkest note trembles in the wood until his breath is gone. He sees his face, distorted in the polished wood. And smiles.

2

'McCulloch.' He says his name aloud. His voice is close in this room. He takes pride in his name; it is the brand name of a chainsaw. He looks at his hands curled about the tube of gunmetal. There is no paint on these hands. They are soft. He once loved to roughen her flesh with his spirit-hardened callouses. He stirs at the thought.

McCulloch is a big man. His muscles have grown soft with the years and he must constantly will them into firming. It makes him squint as though in pain.

In the bedroom the vast bed is unfamiliar. Posts, big pillows, eiderdown. He faces the mirror. The T-shirt is tight; the outline of his nipples shows through. He holds the long barrel before him.

He keeps a careful eye on the space around his image in the glass. Nothing moves in the dimness.

3

Rosemary McCulloch lounges perfectly in the fortified sunlight by the pool. Her thoughts are far from the chunk-chunk of heavy camera shutters and the talk of the photographer. She is possessed by whiteness.

Behind her eyelids there is quivering white. It reminds her of the past; clean, fresh brick pulsating in a street of salmon-pink and terracotta, bright, pale faces of the family just out from England (she remembers the woman's accent as she called for her child – 'Murr-rraaay!'), and the modest chiffon of the bride arriving next door. At dusk the sound of other people's children. Everywhere yards barren with pale coastal sand and harassed-looking runners of buffalo grass.

Sweaty summer nights in white sheets, under his biceps, listening to the sprinklers.

4

A small woman moves among the empty cardboard boxes, and, after a moment's indecision, crosses the glass-strewn floor to the bookcase. She notes, despite herself, that it has not been dusted. She pulls books out, Herbert Kastle, Helen MacInnes – scruffy paperbacks that she drops into the nearest box. *Anna Karenina* she remembers and pulls the cardigan tighter about her as if to secure the memory of debate through the pickets of the fence. *Pure Metaphysical Knowledge* and *New Idea* join the thrillers in the box. Then she scoops out an armful of Simenons and reads the back covers once more and turns and says: 'Remem . . .' and puts a hand to her mouth. Yes, always Maigret, she thinks.

For a few moments she is happy and strong, moving along the shelves, boxing books and discarding more issues of Bilbert Kann's *Pure Metaphysical Knowledge* with resolve. She breathes shallowly, scuffs aside the broken glass.

5

The weapon rears in his hands.

A red geyser issues from an eye socket. The woman staggers.

There is a roar like the heavens opening.

6

Soon after the Housing Commission opened up Playne Street there was an influx of young married couples and English migrants who found deposits for the sandy, treeless blocks, and waited and saw State houses built on them. There were only four styles but designs were often reversed, as if copied in a mirror. Instead of the door of the terracotta double-front opening on the left of the little cement porch, it opened on the right. Tile colours varied.

The McCulloch house, however, was none of the four, and this set it apart. McCulloch, a signwriter, worked at home much of the time and this also held a certain prestige. His wife stayed at home; it was expected of her, but she, like most of the young wives on Playne Street, was happy with her new life in which she had a home that would one day have a garden and a greenhouse and a concrete driveway.

Next door, on the left, lived another young couple. The husband, Phillips, was a clerk with the government; his wife, Ruth Phillips, spent her housecleaning hours planning her new home, nuggeting and polishing the jarrah floorboards each week. Rosemary McCulloch could be sometimes seen standing outside her white house brushing the spiderwebs from the asbestos eaves with a broom, whistling. Her neighbour watched through the pickets.

One afternoon, after the Phillipses had their driveway bitumenized, Ruth Phillips, who was lashing the sandy verge with water to coax the buffalo grass, saw the McCullochs pull in on McCulloch's motorcycle. Flinging dark hair from her eyes, Rosemary McCulloch met her neighbour on the kerb. They spoke shyly, asking girlish questions, laughing in little ragged shreds, often turning to point out things about the two houses, salmon-pink and white.

Thereafter, the two spoke daily – often by the hour – through the fence. They shared cups of Robur tea in each other's kitchen and shopped together in the Phillips' Morris Minor. The two husbands spoke little. Sid Phillips thought conversation with McCulloch was like talking to a small boy; he found himself being patronizing and he tired quickly of talking cars and women. McCulloch spent hours after dark working on his motorcycle with his friends. He thought that Phillips was a bore. Phillips tended to share this view, though his wife did not.

When the Beatles came to Australia, all of them went together; it was Rosemary's idea. For the Phillipses it was deafening and terrifying. For the McCullochs it was like being near the Queen or seeing the Pope. There was a poster of Paul McCartney in their hallway.

The rest of the people living on Playne Street noticed that numbers seven and nine had become close. People told stories of wife-swapping and other titillating atrocities, but there was no truth in them.

Ruth Phillips had a baby, Rosemary McCulloch had a miscarriage and a long depression.

Soon after, McCulloch almost got the contract for a concert tour of Billy Thorpe and the Aztecs, but the promoters decided that they did not like the funny slant he gave to all his letters. Other clients did not like the long shadows he painted into his signs, although most never complained. Many were afraid to offend him.

A woman, a year later, gave birth to a baby with no arms. She and her husband moved from the street. A Yugoslav woman moved in; she was no more popular.

On Sundays 'the kids' came to see McCulloch. They were his old friends from school; he still called them 'the kids'. Rosemary and Ruth, for a year or two, went on picnics on Sundays. Sid Phillips took up golf, despite his loathing it. McCulloch and 'the kids' lifted weights with a transistor bellowing, threw empties over the fence and turned cars all day.

The Phillipses had another son. Rosemary McCulloch gave birth to a son, and the next year, another. The Phillips children grew to be noisy, happy children. The McCulloch boys were quiet. Sullen, some said.

It sometimes occurred to Ruth Phillips that Rosemary was like a young sister. She thought of herself now as a woman, and could not help but feel as though Rosemary was still a girl. Rosemary had a worldly air about her – she knew more about sex than Ruth – but her speech betrayed a schoolgirl's naïvety. Because Rosemary was beautiful and Ruth plain (though her husband did not agree), Ruth Phillips thought of herself as a much older woman. In fact she was five years older.

The children did not play with each other. The Phillips children were wary of the McCullochs and thought the boys were 'a bit slow' because they did not speak much. The McCulloch boys did not seem to have an opinion of the Phillipses, they paid attention to no one.

For her twenty-second birthday, Ruth gave Rosemary a hardcovered edition of *Anna Karenina* which cost a great deal and so seemed to her to be a good book. Rosemary read it slowly at first, then quickly towards the end, and when she had finished, lent it back to Ruth who struggled through the first half, left it for nine weeks, and finished it quickly on a holiday at Dunsborough. Neither of them understood everything in the big, unwieldy book, but the scenes and some of the dialogue became a secret between them. Phillips read *Time* and *National Geographic*, McCulloch read *Phantom* and *Man*.

Rosemary's mother died of cancer and to Rosemary it seemed to happen very quickly. She was quiet and introverted, brooding for several months afterwards. The next year, McCulloch's father suicided, but nothing was ever said about it. The Phillipses, and the others in Playne Street, were not told.

Soon after, a smartly dressed man and woman went to all the doors in the street speaking to people about 'Spiritual Existence' and 'The Sin in What You Eat', selling subscriptions to or stuffing into letterboxes copies of a glossy magazine called *Pure Metaphysical Knowledge*, which some people browsed through as if it was a sales catalogue, and others read carefully for a few pages, then tossed into the rubbish as soon as Sin and Death and Eternal Life appeared in the columns.

Ruth and Rosemary never discussed the magazine, though both read it through independently. Things had already been uneasy between them for months since Phillips had sprayed a hose into McCulloch's carport at two o'clock in the morning a few months before. McCulloch had been tuning his motorcycle. The McCullochs began to behave 'differently'. They were never seen outdoors from Friday night until Sunday morning. No lights were seen in the house. The children became more sullen.

The Phillipses did not know that each Friday morning a new issue of *Pure Metaphysical Knowledge* appeared in the McCullochs' letterbox. The Phillipses puzzled about the strange weekend behaviour of their neighbours and were even more surprised when Rosemary McCulloch asked them to water their lawns and feed their cat for a week.

Rosemary McCulloch did not tell them that they were going to Sydney. Ruth did not ask, and Phillips would rather not have known.

While they were gone, the cat had kittens in the baby's cot. It rained in an unseasonal manner all week. The Phillips children went next door to feed the cats and look at the *Man* magazines in the loungeroom. It was an adventurous week for them.

7

At the window, he sees a woman come off the street past the banks of letterboxes. She pauses at the foot of the stairs and looks up. Her face is lit in the afternoon sun. It is unfamiliar to him. Her face contracts as if in fear, her lips move, and she turns and walks briskly away.

McCulloch waits two minutes. He hears noises through the walls, other people cooking. As he leaves, he slowly tears a poster from the wall. Fragments of cheesecloth and flesh stare at him.

She is working late, he thinks.

He shifts the weight of the weapon from one arm to the other as he moves to the door.

8

He is thinking about her. It bubbles hot within. Crooked notes from her guitar; those first awkward tunes. 'I am learning,' her mouth says. 'No, no,' he is firm. His fingers knot . . . he sings along, stumbling. She smiles. Is it encouragement? Or ridicule? She is laughing!

His brother is a state cricketer!

Her fingers learn to caress the strings. They furrow delicately through dark-backed books that he hates and fears.

He hears the notes as they begin to link with each other, then a gentle strumming, a purring of strings and she is singing.

Please release me, let go,
For I don't love you any more . . .

The voice is cracked and horrible to him.

But his brother is a state cricketer! It warms him for a moment.

9

When the taxi stops outside the agency she bounces across the pavement on her heels and decides that tonight she will ring her sons. Rosemary has not spoken with them for two weeks. She remembers her last conversation with Robbie. How can I explain it? she thinks. She has nothing to tell them, only a twinge of fear, like pain. And sometimes a nauseous guilt she does not understand. Like steamy nights lying awake in the damp sheets, aching, afraid of the blackness that loomed above.

Her son's voice:
Why don't you live here any more?
What's wrong with Dad?
I hate you.
Dad bought me a surfboard today. A six-foot-six Cordingley.
No, Simmy doesn't wanna talk.
Yer lying. He never hurt *us*.
Yes, the toothpaste thing was good. It didn't look like you.
No, I don't wanna talk to you any more; you're tricking me.

10

The carved chest in Ruth Phillips' unsteady hands is made of fragrant wood. She sits on a cardboard carton and opens the lid. Inside, there is a tangle of pearls, beads, balls, bangles.

The pearls untangle themselves first. They are strange to her, their faces like the skin of the moon, mapped with minuscule marks that might be the landmarks of another world. She lays them aside.

She turns a bangle over in her hands. Its tarnished surface gleams dully; there is a smell of incense.

An ugly pair of clip-on earrings with jade settings. Why would someone keep these? she thinks. Oh, Lord, Rosie, she chuckles.

Amid the twisted, blackening chains crouches a red, shapeless stone like a clot of blood. She rolls it in her palms. Yes, had all the best, our Rosie, she thinks.

'The best, Rosie,' she says aloud with a hardness in her voice.

11

The gushing roar as she spins, a perforated hand flung against the wall. Plaster falls like a confetti.

12

McCulloch weaves through the suburban streets, past his house and joins the afternoon traffic on the artery that leads to the city.

The engine of the Fairlane vibrates slowly. He owes a large amount on this car that he will never pay.

He switches the radio on. The news is over; it is ten minutes after four.

He catches his eye in the mirror and acknowledges it with a wink. He senses his brown arm on the sill of the door.

> *Tie a yellow ribbon 'round the old oak tree,*
> *If you still want me,*
> *If you still want me . . .*

He switches the radio off.

'. . . 'round the old oak tree,' he sings brokenly.

13

So what's an E-type Jag? Stuff the bloody Jag! Had enough! Enough filth and greed and stupid talk. Feel this thing corner! Maybe Bilbert (you bastard!) was right . . . Oh, those days of doin' all the right things . . . the way it was supposed to happen . . . Yeah, that was better. But the kids, they still wanted to come over. Still gotta live, you know. And her bloody whingeing.

Stupid, rotten car. Knew it would bust the family up. So, what's it matter? She should know better. Oh, a hard, hard, hard heart. Rotten bitch.

It was that miserable little tit next door what did it in the beginning, asking all them stinking questions – ALL THAT TALK AND BOOKS! *– looking through the fence, doin' filth in the baby's cot. Turned her black inside, she did. Ah, but she went to piss just lookin' at me. Never had it properly in her whole life. And Sidney-kidney-blidney. Agh!*

Suddenly the Fairlane feels cumbersome in his hands. He grinds his palm into the centre of the wheel and the horn squeals.

14

There are more photographs to be taken. Rosemary McCulloch smiles the 'oh, you big man you!' smile and leans on the dummy in the three-piece suit. Later in the afternoon her face will ache from the forced tightening of her lips. She will slick her teeth with Vaseline to keep her mouth from drying out. Her veins will ache from standing.

Cameras chew film.

'C'mon, Rose,' the photographer says smoothly, 'this isn't the old "I did it for Smirnoff" girl I used to know.'

'No?' she says. 'Where did you know her from?'

'C'mon, let's have some life, eh? You know what *life* is, don't you? *Life!* Show them you have life, they want to buy you! They want to eat you!'

'Shit, Charlie, that's sick.'

'Yeah,' says the photographer, sheepishly.

'Anyhow, I don't taste good.'

'No?'

Rosemary tilts her head and catches the mannequin by the pink chin.

'C'mon people, buy me, eat me.'

'Yes, yes,' mutters Charlie.

15

The phone rings. It has not yet been disconnected. It is the executor. Ruth speaks to him for a while. No, he cannot come yet. She needs more time. No, nothing of value, really. Later in the afternoon, yes. She hangs up.

The boxes of cosmetics are open before her, swirling up in a foul, sweet odour. She does not touch anything.

The first time Ruth noticed Rosemary wearing cosmetics was when she needed it to cover lovebites and bruises. Why was it such a show of prowess, she thinks, to show me her big, battered breasts in the privacy of her room? 'This is what he does to me,' she would say with her tongue on her lip.

Then, later, powder and make-up base to cover the welts.

Ruth Phillips remembers the times she ran into her own room, sobbing at the horrible things.

The last year, the plush tones and textures of cosmetics were all that kept her on the billboards.

. . . Much later, no attempt at make-up. No viewing, only a screwed-down lid.

16

Corner from her mouth. Choir of thunder singing.

17

Monoxide fumes ascend in the slanting light. McCulloch fixes his stare on a long, high billboard towering over the intersection. Pedestrians flood across the road. He sees the slit fabric of the dress and the dark recesses of cleavage, bare, smooth skin of the small of the back – and satin, folds and folds of lascivious satin.

    I DID IT FOR SMIRNOFF . . .

'And how many others,' he says quietly to his speedometer.

18

During those bare, safe years, McCulloch was torn between the security that Bilbert Kann gave them in delivering to them the Truth, and hatred of the man (he had filed a lawsuit against him which was later withdrawn) for inflicting upon them the poverty and despair of his Knowledge.

To keep the Sabbath, the house was locked at dusk on Friday nights. They sat and slept and thought, and the children brooded and fought, and the McCullochs read from *Pure Metaphysical Knowledge*:

> . . . *For whatsoever man he be that hath a blemish, he shall not approach: a blind man or a lame, or he that hath a flat nose or anything superfluous* . . .

and spoke words at the ceiling and the slick covers of the source of Truth, and cried and hated and hated and hated.

Meanwhile, the Phillips children called through the

pickets to come and play, safe from answers, safe from playing with 'the horrible McCullochs' who were both 'twice as slow as their old man'.

McCulloch painted signs for the Knowledge Fellowship for a pittance and they gave him specifications, forbade him some images, compelled him to others. Some nights McCulloch sat in the semi-darkness of his workshop and slashed with the brushes at things for himself that he kept under padlock. He threw foreign substances on to the tin flats that he daubed – honey, chocolate, gelatine crystals, chunks of lipstick, petroleum jelly – things that sent the paints into chaos, running out of control, or coagulating stubbornly, or merely losing their colour. The paintings had a dark, uneven terrain, livid – even in twilight – whilst wet, but as dull as dried blood when left to stand a while.

After painting, he would clean off, then go to the blackboard and check off the sins at random. The sins were gleaned from a multiplicity of sources, half-sentences, snippets from the *Koran*, the *Book of Mormon*, *The Himalayas of the Soul*, Leviticus and Deuteronomy, and many personal inspired insertions from Bilbert Kann himself. McCulloch comprehended the literal meanings of a few of them, and did not for a second imagine the textual significance or origins of any.

Be thou to me as thy mother's back . . .

19

Rosemary McCulloch's children were a great disappointment to her; her sons were rough replicas of her husband, and, looking into their wooden faces, she wondered whether or not, in giving birth to them, she had done something wrong. They bit and whined and had the animal instincts of their father, and she pretended to be proud of them as she pretended to be proud of him. But she saw them under his spell, as if the very odours he gave off stunned them into a trance. As they did her.

And she was aware of a vacancy inside her.

She read to them from a *Pure Metaphysical Knowledge*, 'Recite thou in the name of thy Lord who created; created man from clots of blood: Recite thou!' It arrived each Friday from the other side of the continent, from across the desert. Monday they would put the cheque in the mail (THOU SHALT NOT STEAL!). She read from the Truth and was sometimes ashamed. 'Or are ye sure that He who is in Heaven will not send against you a stone-charged whirlwind?' For herself? For not believing? For believing? 'Woe on that day to those charged with imposture!'

20

The wallhangings are mostly photographs by David Hamilton; furtive, voyeuristic, but tranquil. Their apparent innocence puzzles Ruth Phillips. She cannot tell if they are pornographic or beautiful. In one place on the wall there is only a corner, a triangle of paper held to the plaster by a dob of putty. She tries to peel it away, but it sticks to her hands; she cannot rid herself of it and she dirties her dress and leaves smudges on the wall. A feeling of nausea comes upon her.

On a table is a smaller photograph in a light frame. It is Rosemary; she is wearing the cheesecloth blouse and the sensuous pout, brightened by waxy sunlight, like the children in the Hamilton pieces. But this woman is thirty-four years old.

Ruth Phillips puts a hand to her face in confusion.

21

A furrow appears diagonal to the serrated edge of her spine as she slides down, facing, and defacing the discoloured wall.

Thunder has become numbness.

People pass in the street below. No one moves in the corridors. Each shot has no time to cannon off into the distance of silence before it is overtaken by the next.

22

At four twenty McCulloch parks the Fairlane carefully in the midst of the city. His heart moves at a set pace.

He has counted again the sins of the Smirnoff advertisement. He has found seven, though more will come to mind later.

This city has grown with the years since the Beatles came. He is unsure if this is a good thing or a bad thing; no one has yet told him.

23

School has been out for an hour. Bag-swinging children dawdle along footpaths.

McCulloch is proud of his children; if they are in pain he feels it himself. Since babyhood they have played in his paint-tins, fingering the dried, gummy edges; they sprayed their pedal-cars before they could speak properly.

Now they are schoolboys. Robbie truants from school – all classes except Art where he buries himself in a mute world of colours and viscous materials. Simmy, the younger boy, wants to be a weight-lifter. He is thin and asthmatic. McCulloch has encouraged him in his ambition, despite, or perhaps because of, the opposition from his wife.

Teachers worry about Robbie McCulloch's paintings. The distorted figures are unsettling; they are framed – all of them – by arch-like shadows, or the images are visible through foliage or lace curtains. The Art teachers say they are passionate and surrealistic; other teachers say 'Yes, but . . .' Notes home are ignored. The headmaster, a weak little man, has 'gathered some information'. Yes, the boys are disturbed, he has been told by a teacher of Social Studies; their mother has left them only recently. The headmaster has some paintings in his office. He covers them with his academic gown in the corner.

24

Twice today Rosemary has thought of Ruth Phillips. She has not seen her for nine months. It is a year since she left her home. For a few months she dropped in to see Ruth when she knew there would be no one at home next door, and they talked over cups of well-brewed tea. It was difficult to speak in the end; they were so different, and Rosemary was part of a new world.

'Not bad, eh?' she had said, pointing through the little kitchen window to the pink Jaguar, poised in the driveway. 'Not bad for a mother of two, my age,' she said, half-congratulating herself, wanting, at least, confirmation from Ruth.

'Yes,' said Ruth, uncertain, intimidated. 'Yes, you've reached the top, all right.' She said it into the collar of her dowdy gown.

The second time Rosemary went back they tried to talk about the past, but Rosemary was embracing what Ruth feared the most; the future.

The last visit, Rosemary was drunk. She slewed the Jaguar into the drive, crushing the heads of the roses growing along the edge.

'You've gotta help me, Ruthie,' she said. 'He's after me. I think he's gonna kill me.'

'Calm down, Rosemary,' Ruth said.

'He's got a gun.' This was true; he had an American service weapon. A number of people living on Playne Street knew that he had it. He told people about it; it brought him a great deal of respect.

But Ruth Phillips was irritated.

'Go back to your flat,' she almost spat the last word, 'and get yourself a good sleep.' She deplored drunkenness; it made people say things they didn't mean.

Rosemary decides that she will ring Ruth. She yearns for her soft, reassuring voice from the other world. She wishes she could tell Ruth some things. She's a good stick, she thinks.

Sometimes it occurs to her that she is older than Ruth. Despite herself, she longs for the days when they were both new brides and new friends. She wonders if those times were so good because she did not know certain things.

Rosemary's attention is distracted from her work. She is hearing her voice and Ruth's voice: '. . . *you've got a lovely shoulder to cry on, Ruth love,*' *pulling down her mini.* 'You too, love,' *Ruth says, dripping tears that smudge the polish of her floorboards.*

25

Ruth Phillips lingers over the furniture in the flat. Rosemary's chairs are delicate, with soft curves and cushions and dark, rich wood, not the strong vinyl and
wipe-clean surfaces of the stuff in her own house. In her place things are cheap and useful, and nothing has changed since 1964. Tasteless old Ruth, she thinks, flopping into an armchair. She sits a while, becoming dispirited, before getting up to stack it all by the door.

26

An arm lifts as it is struck, the wall vibrates. And the endless thunder.

People are screaming, but their voices are smothered in the roar.

27

Office workers streaming out of shadowy buildings do not notice the automatic rifle that McCulloch is carrying by his side in the rush, even though it enters and leaves the vision of scores of them. It is twenty-five minutes past four and they are going home. McCulloch pushes against the surge and enters the sleek glass doors. Inside, carpet muffles all movement, and seems to exude a narcotic breath which tempts him to lie down and go to sleep in its burgundy pile.

Young women, some of whom he recognizes from places he cannot recall, walk past him from the lift. One woman, a tall, black, lithe creature, turns her head in surprise.

Weep ye that lie down with other tribes and with animals...

McCulloch walks towards the potted palms near the lift.

28

Billboards, plaques, all signs attract McCulloch's attention. He has been a signwriter since the age of sixteen. He was a signwriter when he was married. He is a signwriter now: it says so in the telephone directory below his name, though he has not had a client for almost eight months. No one recommends him; he is lazy, they say, late, they say, and he does not always paint what he is asked.

The most recent thing he has painted is on the wall at home in Playne Street. It is a long piece of masonite with a white background and big, red, Gothic letters. It says:

GOD IS LOVE

The staccato words puzzle him. He put them there to remind his children and himself. Beneath the bold letters, niggled pencil lines show through. Even though he had not thought of God or Love for some time, he had suddenly been seized by the idea after his wife left him. She left a note:

> *I do not love Bilbert Kann's God. I do not know him. I never knew him. I don't love you, either, though I know you only too well. I don't think I've ever loved you, really. I have spent my whole life pretending. No more pretending. I have finished pretending. I have. You can't even pretend. That's what you are like.*

He crushed it in his fist and brought his hand down on to

the Laminex with some force. He went to work quickly, in fright, splashing on the primer.

29

The session is finished. Rosemary sits with some other girls in the studio drinking coffee, listening to their talks of cruises to Noumea and jobs on television quiz shows. Some even talk about getting married, though they are wary around Rosemary. They treat her with a respect for her position, the most enviable in the business at the moment, and resentment for her age and her sudden ascent.

Rosemary is in great demand. People want to see a woman who has had children, who has married and experienced life, who is both homely and glamorous, voluptuous in her ripeness.

As a new wife Rosemary was an object of interest, to herself, her husband, and her husband's friends. She lived an endless procession of Sunday afternoons when her husband 'had the boys over'. They drank beer and ogled her, McCulloch displaying her like a sleek new road-machine, fanning their heat, their stares and catcalls, coaxing them to stay longer, to come again. He knew they liked to come to his place. After all, they were his best mates. In later years, they began to lose interest, when McCulloch began to mutter about the Meaning of Life and the Tithing of Time, so he asked her, begged her, sometimes, to wear clothes that were more daring. He dressed her to look like Nancy Sinatra. They patted her and they were all great friends. She loved those beery afternoons because they gave her an outlet after the dreary Sabbath, and she enjoyed the attention. Afterwards she was always left with an elusive nausea, as if she might throw up something that lurked deep inside her, and she took a sleeping tablet and dreamed till morning whereupon she rose with a clear head and not even a dim memory of what she had dreamt.

She listens to the girls' self-conscious talk.

Rosemary McCulloch is a model. She is the woman-model. She gives life to clothes, libido to car bonnets, meaning to vodka. She sets the pace for mothers and daughters who want to be like her.

Her husband is haunted by her reproductions, and her sons have learnt to hate her.

30

The wardrobes are fragrant with the smell of Rosemary's perfumes and the odours of her body. Ruth Phillips recalls the smells from when they gardened and jogged together. They tried hard, then, to disguise and dispel their body odours. They tried roll-ons, spray-ons, dab-ons, and stick-ons. As she grew older, Ruth tired of trying, and she spent less time worrying about her appearance. Phillips grew accustomed to her odour, and had said, once, that he even liked it, so she saw no need to bother.

Rosemary pursued deodorants; she could not afford to have a smell of her own. But she had one, nevertheless. Ruth recognizes and remembers it.

'Funny thing to think of,' she says aloud.

She feels the fabrics of pullovers and cardigans, lingering over the older, less fashionable things that smell of dowdy innocence. Chenille brushes between her fingers. Old jeans, faded and patched, are difficult to fold into the box.

Ruth Phillips feels old.

31

The bullet that enters the chest sounds like an old football being kicked two doors away.

32

McCulloch is light-headed with the feeling of ascent. Lighted numbers pop and ping above his head. If he was alone in the lift he would jump to see if the floor would overtake him.

He is soaring.

The woman beside him is more alarmed by his breathing than by the stock of the weapon brushing against her thick hip.

33

On a summer evening McCulloch came home with a trunk full of costumes. He dressed up and faked magic tricks for his boys who were thrilled at the colours, half-believing. He pulled caps from false-walled boxes and knitting needles from handkerchiefs. His wife acted along with him, despite herself. She could see it was good for the children and for him. He had been upset of late, despairing at the admonishments they had received in the mail from Sydney. They had no money and their faith had weakened. Kann was calling them to the half-completed Opera House and they refused. McCulloch had nightmares.

She played along with the games. The boys made costumes. There were others in the trunk.

34

As she sips coffee in the hubbub, Rosemary thinks also of her eldest son, Robbie. She loves him; he is her own flesh and blood, like a piece cut from her, but she has never liked him. She is honest about this. So honest that she once told Ruth Phillips whose face darkened with confusion and discomfort.

'Look, it's just the way it is,' she said. 'I can't explain it properly. You know what he's like.'

'But he's your child,' Ruth said, always grateful that Robbie McCulloch was not hers.

Robbie McCulloch has a 'speech problem'. He hardly spoke until his second year at school. He shows no affection. Sometimes he smiles at his father.

There were times when Rosemary believed that she had been cursed with such a son because of the manner in which he had been conceived. McCulloch copulated with her as if she was a carcass from an abattoir. At first she wept at the sounds he made and the things he made her do when sex was something new to her, something frightening and exciting. But she soon learned the techniques of sex he taught her: endurance, agility, and a measure of dramatic exaggeration. She loved to shock 'poor Ruthie Phillips' who understood little of sexual matters. Ruth sometimes introduced The Right Thing and God to their discussions about sex which she endured. But she knew less about God than she did about sex, and cared still less. She had a home to take care of and had little time for either. She also spoke of Love, but it was a puzzling subject.

35

Ruth Phillips, when she notices something odd about the underwear she is refolding, suddenly puts it down and sits on the floor. A cry escapes her. She sits, mute, for a few minutes until her mind clears. Then she gets up again and stuffs all the torn, soiled, alien garments into a box and runs to the bathroom to wash her hands and splash her face.

It leaves her with a light head. Her stomach tolls.

36

He aims where it gives him most pleasure and the lower half quivers again. He is alone in the room with her and the choir in his ears.

37

There is no one in the corridor down which he is stalking. He feels as though his feet are not even touching the ground, though they leave heavy prints in the pile. Photographs on the walls. Pieces of her float by. They shower him, spurring him so he glides faster.

38

In 1969 McCulloch's father committed suicide. He was a big man, like his son, who often spent hours, days even, contemplating, brooding about things that mattered to him but of which he never spoke. He was a cattleman who owned big land in the North. Regularly, he left the staff at the station homestead (his wife, an ex-barmaid from

Boulder, had died some years before) and spent two or three days in the bush. On his last day he drove out into the heartlands and shot himself. Birds and animals gradually robbed him of his flesh and he was identified, months later, by his yellow teeth. He was a lapsed Methodist. He grieved constantly over his son's becoming 'a half-Jehovwit-Latter-Day-Saturday-Cultist', and he thought that worse even than the 'useless, ignorant nothing' his son had been before the cultists had knocked on his door. He had never ceased to grieve for his wife who had died suddenly of a stroke. Also, he was bored and scared. He felt bad things about his son, though he did not believe too strongly in omens because, even if lapsed, he was still a Methodist.

The station staff buried his shabby remains after the inquest, on the station, and he was bought along with the place when his son quickly sold it.

39

Pieces fly at him. He is flying. Into pieces.

40

Her second son, Simmy, is as much of a disappointment to Rosemary as Robbie. He has a prominent brow that divides above his nose like the swelling from a boxing blow. He speaks without difficulty but he is totally expressionless; his words are like the monosyllables of a plastic doll. His cheeks are bright, as if rouged; his teeth are sturdy and white, like his father's. When he uses barbells he wheezes, a clicking hiss deep in his chest. He will never lift weights properly.

Rosemary remembers the first words he spoke. The

da-da-da-da-da was as accentless and unremitting as a heartbeat.

Simmy is a product of the 1965 Multiplication for the End. But there had been no End, thus far.

During her second pregnancy, Rosemary often stood naked before the mirror to see the evidence of her swelling. She watched each day, minutely aware that she was becoming two people. She knew very little of either of them. Afterwards her flaccid torso revolted her. Her baby disappointed her, and the image of an unkempt, dumpy woman before her in the mirror added to her depression.

Her second son gained his name from the author of a book Rosemary and her friend had read years ago: *Red Lights*. He has never been told this. It is unlikely that he would understand or show interest.

She cannot help but see Neanderthal in him.

41

Stalks through the carpet . . .

42

Ruth opens the trunk with a gasp. Slowly, she draws out the top garment. In a few moments she understands what it is.

'*Spiderman*,' she says, remembering her children's comics. It is sparking something in her memory; a stone striking metal. Snakeskin, long strips of it, comes out. It is smooth and evil-looking. A schoolcap. A pair of grey shorts like her sons wear; she shudders. She digs into the voluminous box. Moons; a magician's outfit. A horse's head, creased and rubbery, bares its teeth. Her hand touches something coarse. She pulls gingerly and what she pulls out she cannot identify for a few seconds until she comes to the head and the hands; it is an ape suit.

'Oh,' she murmurs, half in recognition, half in fright. She is not angry yet, because she is not allowing herself the pain of understanding. Somewhere in her mind is a vivid memory she refuses to see.

She stands at the broken window watching traffic easing out of the city into the suburbs.

> *Spiderman, spiderman,*
> *does whatever a spider can . . .*

She remembers it from television, glad she is remembering that which is of limited importance. Ruth Phillips refuses to recall forty-five seconds of her life. It is this:

. . . She is looking through the pickets, idly. She sees a man dressed gaudily in red, white, and blue with knee-length boots and a cape. He has a helmet on his head. Stars cling to all his garments. On the concrete paving there is another figure sprawled, in bountiful skirts, with a hat and white wooden clogs like a china doll. Above the squirming doll is the man with his shield brandished . . . then there is nothing as the pickets recede.

'Captain America waves his mighty shield,' she says. She puts the winged helmet aside, gazes at the righteous pyramid the 'A' makes, embossed on the brow. Her mind convulses, free of her. She sobs, remembering. He's polluted her, she thinks, it's in *her* now, she's tainted even now when she's dead. Can't she be free of him?

Everywhere she smells sickness and she is hopeless, perfectly ineffectual. God, I've always been useless to her, useless to myself, she thinks through a falling curtain of tears. She remembers, irrational with guilt and hysteria, that she and her brothers pulled the limbs from dolls and inverted their puckers with a thumb inside their heads. They always reassembled them, later, though. But the thought ceases to comfort her.

'Waves his mighty bloody shield.'

43

Four twenty-nine . . .

44

A shoulder strap dematerializes as the flesh beneath it shatters into white pieces that quickly shade over.

Rosemary is in the burgundy carpet, broken face buried in its scent. Once, she might have imagined this roar to be the God of Bilbert Kann descending on the Opera House with his business associates. But it is a roar of vacancy and vacuum, and, in any case, she does not hear it.

45

. . . and fifty-eight seconds.

46

At exactly four thirty by the not-always-defective clock in the corridor (a joke shared by the models who work here; they often wish it was defective more often), McCulloch confronts the glass doors and watches them open obediently without his touching them. He feels as if he is expected and welcome. A hero's welcome, he thinks. The glass clicks together in a frigid union behind him.

47

Bilbert Kann left the United States of America after a scandal involving his advertising company and certain members of the Senate. He resurfaced in Australia soon afterwards to take part in the optimistic new growth of the early 1960s.

Many who knew him then described him as a prophetic businessman. He understood the nature of people. With this understanding he discovered and developed a marketable god which he promoted in a glossy magazine, *Pure Metaphysical Knowledge*. His god, as the market-culture demanded, was a low-profile, uninterfering one. People observed certain codes and legalities and Kann's god kept out of their way. No one but Kann ever met this god. He had a blueprint for him in his safe, a patent, an artist's impression, and a volume of inspired writings. Kann's disciples were grateful for a mediator; it spared them a great deal of effort and discomfort to have a go-between.

Kann aimed at the Lowest Common Denominator. He borrowed and patched until he came up with a vague but versatile image.

Since 63 AD, he maintained, no True Religion had been preached. 'God has revealed himself to me,' he said on 24 December 1959. Ten years, fifteen years later, he had begun to believe it himself. It was a logical thing to happen.

In the first national issue of his magazine he gave ten or more commandments, and mated those with clipped phrases from fashionable and forgotten religious canons. He found that Australians were naturally legalistic and therefore eager to subscribe to the Worldwide Fellowship and pay tithes.

In a very few years, the Fellowship was truly worldwide. In 1971 when he had five hundred thousand subscribers in Australia alone, he predicted the End of the World within the year, and located the Divine Appearance at the yet incomplete Opera House in Sydney. Fifteen thousand people gathered, many of them staying in hotels operated by Kann's syndicate. The crowd included many entertained spectators. The sun rose and set. At length, the scoffing crowds went home or to the airport to fly home. As the hotdog stands were dismantled, Bilbert Kann and his son Macabee-Dowell told the press and television reporters that God had seen the leaden hearts of his people and rebuked Earth by postponing his Coming.

The next year Macabee-Dowell slipped the country with one of his father's wives and a considerable fortune and was publicly denounced. After two more false second comings and a tightening of monetary rules, subscriptions waned and many ex-disciples sought legal advice. Late in 1974, Kann shifted his assets to European banks. In 1975 he moved to South Africa where his racial legalities were highly marketable. He was assassinated by black youths during a tour of an industrial township in the same year. In 1976 his son founded a syndicate of drive-in churches across the United States of America. He foresaw a great resurgence of profitable legalism in the country within years. He died of cancer in Utah during the presidency of Jimmy Carter in 1979.

48

Rosemary is thinking of soft light and the smell of incense. She is thinking of her lover, a woman who is mute. They have been in love for two months. Her lover will sit on the edge of the bed and watch Rosemary perform. Rosemary sings and dances for her, mimes, reads poetry to her, nuzzles her, and lies in bed with her all Saturday, every weekend. This is the most secret thing in her life. Her husband does not know; he will never find out.

At times, in bed with her sleeping mute lover, Rosemary is bound by a weight of melancholy she does not understand. Other times, it is a prickling violence. She gazes out through the open window of her flat at the back awning of sky and feels its inky vastness descending upon her.

Her lover does not know she is a model. This is a novelty for Rosemary; she is entertained by innocence. Her lover stays more nights now. Rosemary is fascinated by her expressive face, the softness of her body, the absence of the brutality Rosemary fears and often feels within herself. She mimes with her lover; the woman is silent as a soft doll.

With some of her heart Rosemary wishes to tell Ruth Phillips about her new friend, but she can no longer tell anyone. And the secrecy is much of the thrill.

Suddenly, jerkily, she puts down her coffee cup and decides she *will* ring Ruth Phillips, and yes, she will tell her. It would only be ... right ... she thinks without conviction.

And tonight, she thinks, I'll be with my lover who makes no sound.

49

GOD IS LOVE!

It shouts at him; he withholds the urge to run screaming. His biceps quake.

50

Ruth Phillips' sobbing rises to a moan as she uncovers the alien apparatus. She has never seen a dildo before, but she understands its intent; the straps with it upset her more. She finds oily jars and jellies and some pornographic photographs of women as well as dark, heavy leather garments thick with the concentrated stench of mildew and sweat. The floor is now carpeted with costumes and the odours overcome her. She is driven to her knees and she cries out.

'No! No! It's not true!' But she knows she is mocking herself. She nods, acknowledging something she does not understand. She realizes what she does not know. Have I ever met Rosie McCulloch? she asks herself. She spins inwardly. She is uncertain about who she has ever known.

She collapses in a heap with a photograph in her fist.

51

Clicks together, like a snip.

52

The last image in Rosemary's conscious existence is a rose enveloping the world with its cool, impenetrable petals. She is gone, but her twisted body is undeniably present, mutilated on the floor. Another eruption gives it a semblance of life, but the deception is momentary as the pelvis quivers. Her body is dead.

53

I swear by the declining day,
Verily, man's lot is cast amid destruction . . .

He shakes his head. The pink Jaguar knifes into him, long, glistening, sleek.

54

And before him is his wife Rosemary McCulloch of Smirnoff fame who passes the receptionist's desk and whose eyes recoil as their gazes meet. A sharp intake of her breath. McCulloch has the weapon before him. He brandishes it at her. She does not move. He takes careful aim and triggers its unalterable mechanism.

55

In the last seconds before entering the reception office, McCulloch has discarded all excuses. There is no thought of Sin or God or Truth in his mind. These are things he no longer needs. He can think of nothing but the pink Jaguar roaring, leaving and entering his vision with spurts of speed. He sees his wife in all poses in it. He sees the boys pawing it with sighs of wonder, looking into her face. He sees Rosemary in an aura of pink reflection. 'Well, look what I got,' she says sneering. He sees her packing. Things she has paid for. Scribbling in the jotter on the Laminex table. He sees himself. Smashing furniture against the white wall and Paul McCartney.

He could feel her behind him as he ran out with the axe. Felt her breath teeming against his bare back as she clung on to him with her nails and teeth as he smashed the headlights and struck the long, pink nose and skittered windscreen glass and pierced the pouting rouged cheek of the fender and saw steam, and the car expired audibly. The removal men looked on with amusement.

The bloody Jag! he thinks. Aaaaah! It makes him shudder with sickness. Her solid-framed, immovable, luxuriant reproductions beam from the walls and hound him. He flexes forward, aware again, of flight.

His sons hate him for the Jaguar.

He hears the rending of metal and he feels the unused muscles creaking within him. He flexes forward, aware again, of flight.

'God will—' he begins, but remembers he has no need of God and he surges on to do some kind of duty.

56

There are times when Rosemary McCulloch can look back on the hardest period of her life with a sort of longing. In the first years of Membership and Fellowship, she spent many hours locked away with her young children. At times they mimicked her; they listened to her stories. They acknowledged her presence when she shared her portion of food with them. They sat with her on the floor without furniture and listened, like her, to McCulloch's puzzled intonations from the Law. Perhaps they shared a stubbornness. They dozed while McCulloch called with staged enthusiasm and tried to feel his soul move. Perhaps, too, they felt his hate soaking everything, but they were young.

When Rosemary feels these things she is usually alone in her flat and she is half drunk with vodka. It is poor consolation. Even Ruth Phillips seems a spectre to her. She looks for her strong, happy face in the faces of her mute lover, but none of her lover's masks will fit.

She knows she can never look back on these things for help. She feels the still resilient firmness of her body, feels her lover responding to it, and knows that she still lives. It is my future, she says to her mute lover who caresses her.

She leaves the room. No, I will not ring Ruthie, she muses. She won't even begin to understand. Anyway, it's all over between us. Come on, Rosie, don't be a baby. She is still undecided about a phonecall to the boys. She is waiting for a call from the insurance people to see if her car is worth salvaging.

The buzzer rings. The receptionist is in the toilet. Rosemary knows this, and to help, she goes to the desk for her.

57

The executor of the will is due in an hour and a half. Ruth Phillips has been crying. Now she is in control. She is thinking clearly. She steps outside and looks into the rear courtyard near the half dozen parked cars of the other tenants. In the corner of the shaded yard is a blackened incinerator. She watches it for a few moments. A snake of smoke escapes it. Somebody is burning something already.

She walks through the boxes she has packed: books, jewellery, cosmetics, wallhangings, clothing, underwear, costumes and sexual tools. She has stuffed all the repugnant things into one box. She hefts it to her waist and begins towards the door. Before she reaches it, she stops and drops the box at her feet. It seems deceitful, somehow, to burn those things she does not like to remember. Now that she knows a great deal about her friend, Rosemary McCulloch, she is tempted to withdraw to the image she has held previously.

But in a surge of relief and honesty, and thinking of the children that she never liked, she takes the box to the door to fulfil what her mind will do in any case.

58

She sits, truly grieving, waiting for the executioner to inspect with expertise and calculation. She takes up *Anna Karenina* from the box, aware of the smell of plastics burning, and realizes that she remembers nothing of it; not a thing.

Inside the cover is scrawled in pencil:

> *In a mirror*
> *you can only see your front*
> *and what's behind you.*

She does not remember the inscription. It does not surprise her, though. The book's musty odour is repulsive to her.

59

The receptionist runs blindly in from the toilet. There has been a long silence. The others are back in the studio, hiding, but she does not know this.

She screams when she sees the bloodied mess before her and she reels as McCulloch rises from his chair in fright.

The bullet hits the metal frame of a photograph and ricochets.

The receptionist falls as if the burgundy carpet has been pulled from beneath her. Blood issues from a small wound in her ankle. She screams. And screams. And screams.

McCulloch sits again; the thick barrel between his knees. He shifts in his seat and reaches for a fashion magazine.

60

There were ten shots. Police arrived at five o'clock. They pushed through the crowd and made an arrest and called an ambulance.

PICADOR
...& more

Talk about books with us, our authors, other readers, bloggers, booksellers and others at www.picador.com

You can also:

- find out what's new at Picador
- read extracts from recently published books
- listen to interviews with our authors
- get exclusive special offers and enter competitions